Billionaire by Design

By

Dee Markwith

Contents

Chapter One

"What's going on?" Zane Talbot leaned forward and asked his driver as the limousine suddenly coasted into the parking lot of the fast food joint. A stop at *Family Burger* definitely wasn't on the agenda, and he was already running late as it was.

"Friggin' thing just died on me," Carl, his chauffeur of ten years, muttered as the vehicle rolled to a stop. "Check engine light's on," he added in his familiar grizzled voice.

"Shit," Zane sighed, sinking back into his seat. He suspected the giant pothole Carl had cruised over with reckless abandonment only moments earlier was to blame, but knew reprimanding the aging man wouldn't help their current situation. Carl had always served him well, but it was abundantly clear that his eyesight had taken a turn for the worse in recent months.

Zane, a strikingly handsome man in his mid-thirties, stole a glance at his wristwatch with his piercing blue eyes. His gold Rolex confirmed what he already knew: there was no way he was going to make this meeting. Without hesitation, he pulled his cell phone from the breast pocket of his black Armani suit and dialed his secretary. As the founder and president of *Enterprise*

Marketing, he recognized that his presence wasn't genuinely required for this meeting. An old client wanted to discuss a new business strategy, and as much as he would like to be there, he was fully aware that Phil Miller, his right-hand man and trusted confidant, would manage just fine without him.

"Enterprise Marketing, Mr. Talbot's office. How can I help you?" his secretary's chipper voice answered after the third ring.

"Sheryl, it's Zane," his deep, commanding voice sounded into his phone. "Do me a favor and shoot Phil a message. Tell him the company cars are on the fritz, and I won't be able to make it to the Eegee's meeting today."

"Oh, I'm so sorry to hear that," Sheryl said apologetically. "I'll pass the message along to Mr. Miller. He just headed into the conference room."

"Yeah, I figured he was about to start, so I didn't bother texting him. Tell him I'll be back when I can," Zane replied as he watched Carl pop the hood of the car and step outside to take a peek underneath it.

"Okay, Mr. Talbot. Anything else I can assist you with?"

"No, but thank you, Sheryl," he responded politely despite his frustration. *Eegee's* was a popular local restaurant chain with plans to expand, and he knew a lot about this meeting. He reminded himself of Phil's competency and assured himself that the *Eegee's* account was in good hands. He'd hired Phil fresh out of college five years earlier, and the guy has proven to be a valuable asset to his growing firm. Tucson was a big city, and he was still twenty minutes away from the office. Phil, his client relations manager, would have to field this one on his own.

Ending the call and placing his phone back in his jacket pocket, he glanced out the windshield where Carl was no longer visible thanks to the limousine's raised hood. He turned his attention out his tinted window to the parking lot they'd stalled out in, letting out a faint chuckle as he realized where the wounded car had died.

"I'll be damned," he grinned, rolling his window down slightly. *Family Burger* was another local restaurant chain that had accrued a loyal following over the years. However, they hadn't expanded their business in quite some time, and this location was showing its age. The building looked run down, and the storefront window signage was mostly done by hand —

something Zane Talbot had always been quite vocal against. He believed it cheapened the appearance of a business and had urged his clients to steer clear of it in favor of professionally printed signs. These signs, however, were adorned with artwork that was actually quite impressive. Somebody had painstakingly drawn cheeseburgers, fries, and fountain soda cups on them in what must have taken many hours. The degree of effort sunk into these pieces was not lost on him.

Stepping out of the car and into the dry desert heat, Zane used a big hand to shield his eyes from the bright sky as he looked up at the *Family Burger* logo that was decaying on the building's roof.

The lettering, now yellowed from years of abuse by the powerful Tucson sun, felt like an old friend. Not only had he grown up in this sprawling city and had many a childhood meal at this family-owned burger joint, but it was also one of the first businesses his marketing firm had scored when he'd launched it twelve years earlier.

He'd been only twenty-two years old then, and numerous newspaper and magazine articles had referred to him as a savant with an uncanny ability to create marketing strategies that people could relate to. He had a natural ability to visualize creative logos and concoct catchy slogans that were pleasing to both producers and consumers. Through persistence and hard work, he'd managed to secure fifteen impressive clients by the time he was only twenty-five, and as the numbers grew, he was forced to hire additional staff. Now, a decade later, his firm employed fifty people and boasted close to one hundred and twenty clients ranging from small to large.

As he surveyed the worn building, he realized that his firm hadn't had many meetings with *Family Burger* in recent years. It pained him to see the restaurant looking so beaten since the excellent food and service had helped the business achieve a moderate degree of local success over the decades. With ten locations across the city, they'd become a staple of Tucson, but their growth had seemingly fizzled out through no fault of his firm.

A string of profanity returned his focus to the limousine, where Carl was bent over the vehicle's engine with a look of anger.

"Goddamn thing!" he growled as he shook his head.

"No luck?" Zane asked flatly.

"I got no idea what's wrong with it!" Carl shot back, throwing up his hands in defeat. Zane once again found himself staring at the run-down restaurant with its handwritten promotional signs taped to its windows.

"Call a tow," he replied calmly while he headed towards the building, "and I'll have the company send another car."

"Where you goin'?" he heard Carl ask from behind him.

"To grab some lunch!" Zane laughed, continuing towards *Family Burger's* entrance. "You want anything?" he offered in afterthought.

"Hook me up with some fries!" Carl hollered as the restaurant's door closed behind him.

Chapter Two

"What's the status of order fifty-seven?" Jenna shouted while she mindlessly wiped down the restaurant's front counter.

"Coming right up!" a male voice answered from the back.

Michael, who'd been scheduled to man the grill that afternoon, rushed to the front to hand the waiting customer a brown bag containing two piping-hot cheeseburgers. He shot Jenna a friendly smile on his way back to his station, and she returned it as she continued cleaning the counter.

At twenty-four years old, the last thing Jenna Parker ever envisioned was working at a fast food joint in Tucson, Arizona. Originally from New York City, she'd moved to the desert four years earlier to build a better life for herself. It was hard leaving her family behind, but she'd been told countless times that the Southwest's wide, open space and dry air would be much better for her asthma. That had actually proven true, but she'd had other reasons for the move as well. Growing up in a rough neighborhood in Brooklyn, she'd watched all three of her brothers succumb to gang life. One had been gunned down outside a club eight years earlier, one had been sentenced to ten years in prison for armed robbery, and the other... well, it was just a matter of time before he wound up dead or in prison.

As the youngest of the four, her father had skipped out on them just after she was born. Her mother rarely talked about him, but Jenna suspected he may have left her for another woman. Unlike her brothers, she avoided trouble at all costs by keeping her nose buried in either a book or her sketchpad. Reading and artwork were her escape, and from an early age, she dreamed of someday moving far away from the neighborhood she'd watched suck the life out of so many people.

It was a sinkhole of negativity, but it was the best her mother could do, having been left alone to raise four children. More than a few times, she'd heard murmurs that her mom had resorted to prostitution to keep food on the table, but she chose to believe that couldn't be true.

Most of her female friends had dropped out of high school after allowing themselves to be smooth-talked and subsequently knocked up by the wrong men, but Jenna vowed that would never happen to her. She'd never allowed herself to become another inner-city statistic and kept her focus aimed at her studies. She'd proudly graduated at the top of her class and planned on using the scholarship she'd been awarded to further her education. Straight out of high school, Jenna took a full-time job at a local bodega, knowing that every penny she saved would be going towards her inevitable move. In her downtime, her cheap tablet replaced her sketchbook as she developed a penchant for graphic art.

Although it pained her to do it, she used some of the money she'd stashed away for her move to buy herself a desktop computer. She justified it as an investment since it was essential to continue pursuing her digital artwork. She spent her evenings teaching herself Photoshop and honing her skills, relieved by how supportive her mother was of her new-found passion.

In the two years she worked at the bodega, the small store got robbed by gunpoint on three separate occasions, two of which she'd been present for. After having a masked assailant shout demands at her while waving a pistol in her face for a second time, she collected her final paycheck and called it quits. She would have liked to have saved up a bit more money but knew she had enough to finally move out of the city if she had budgeted just right. Having heard nothing but good things about the Southwest's climate and scenic views, she enrolled at The University of Arizona to major in graphic design after a fair degree of research. She packed all her belongings into her beat-up 1992 Ford Tempo and prayed that it had enough life left to get her across the country. With a heavy heart, she said her goodbyes to her mother and remaining brother before starting a new, hopefully better, chapter in her life.

As smart as she was, she kicked herself for believing her old car could make the 2,400-mile drive without issue. Along the way, she had to replace its starter, alternator, one headlight, four brake pads, and a blown tire.

She hadn't accounted for such unexpected expenses, and by the time she rolled into Tucson. She had less than two hundred dollars left to her name. She had to fight back tears as she pawned the sterling silver necklace her grandmother had given her shortly before her death, and she only managed to score eighty dollars for it.

She had slept in her car the first two nights, having spent her days scouring the help wanted section of the *Arizona Daily Star* newspaper and calling as many places as she could. When she stopped by *Family Burger* on her third day hoping to find a cheap meal, the "Now Hiring" sign taped to the back-lit menu behind the counter seemed like an act of divine intervention. Fast food wasn't her first choice, but given her circumstances, she couldn't exactly be picky. Not many places were chomping to hire a poor young black girl from the ghetto.

As luck would have it, the manager happened to be on duty and could interview her on the spot, thanks to business being slow. He was a short, friendly Mexican man, and the two instantly liked one another. She was completely honest about her situation, and when he learned that she could begin work immediately, he welcomed her aboard and scheduled her to start the very next day.

At 5'9" with long legs, ample breasts, and a toned body, Jenna had grown accustomed to being told she was beautiful. She remained modest, however, and was always dismissive of the compliments. She certainly didn't feel very attractive after traveling for days and having slept in her car for two sweltering nights. The summer heat had been brutal, and even if her clunker of a vehicle had air conditioning, she couldn't have afforded the gas needed to enjoy it. She was surprised *Family Burger* had been so quick to hire her and counted her blessings as she checked into the cheapest motel she could find to take a much-needed shower and rest on an actual bed.

Family Burger was meant to be a stepping stone, a temporary job to tide her over until something better came along. Yet, they treated her so well that she found herself still employed four years later and had worked her way up to assistant manager.

The pay wasn't great, but enough to scrape by and she'd settled into a small apartment with a fellow employee nearby. Her schooling was going quite well, and the restaurant had been very accommodating in working around her academic schedule. Her coworker and new roommate, Leigh, had become a close friend and the only real support system she had out West.

In the four years she'd worked for *Family Burger*, she'd never seen anything quite like this. Hearing the restaurant's entrance chime, she looked up to see a strikingly handsome man in a solid black business suit striding across the lobby toward her.

She guessed his height to be around 6'4", and he radiated a confidence that attracted her like a magnet. As he drew closer, his baby blue eyes took her breath away, and not a single strand of his long, black hair was out of place. Over his shoulder, she could see a stretch limousine in the parking lot, and it didn't take much deduction to figure out who it belonged to. This exemplary man definitely looked out of place in a fast food joint, and he seemed as though he'd be much more comfortable in a posh five-star restaurant. His content grin, however, suggested he felt right at home in this second-rate establishment.

As he stood before her at the counter, his perfect smile widening and kindness in his eyes, she realized with embarrassment that she'd been staring at him since the moment he'd stepped foot in the restaurant. She quickly tossed aside the rag she'd been using to wipe down the counter and regained her composure.

"Welcome to Family Burger, where you're part of our family! What can we make you?" she asked, returning his smile.

"Ah, let me see..." he trailed off, staring at the menu. After a few seconds, he added, "Sorry, I haven't been here in a while."

"You don't look like you've *ever* been here," she chuckled as she ran her eyes down his expensive suit. Her comment clearly caught him off guard, and after a momentary pause, his eyes widened as he patted his jacket.

"Ah, yes," he laughed, also looking down at his outfit. "Believe it or not, I came here quite often when I was a kid."

"You a lawyer or something?" she prodded, trying her best to hide her urban patois from this well-spoken and obviously successful man.

"No. Even worse. Marketing," he joked.

"Well, you must be damn good at it," she shot back while admiring his attire again.

"Eh, I have my moments. My staff really deserves the credit," he replied as his eyes returned to the menu.

"You run your own company?" Jenna asked, fidgeting with the corners of the register. She couldn't help but be intrigued by this man who exuded wealth and power, and he was undeniably easy on the eyes.

"I do. Enterprise Marketing. This place is actually one of our clients. Oh, and I'll have a number four with a Diet Coke... to go."

"You mean you make commercials for Family Burger?" she questioned, raising her brow as she punched in his order.

"Some, yes. I actually created the whole 'Welcome to the Family' campaign many years ago," he replied while pulling his black leather wallet from his back pocket.

"I love that slogan! I thought you said you weren't good?"

"As I said, that was many years ago. Is Family Burger a national chain yet?" he laughed.

"Good point," Jenna giggled in return. Family Burger had opened their tenth restaurant six years earlier and hadn't expanded since.

"Oh, hell, can you add on an order of medium fries for my driver out there?" he asked as he pointed over his shoulder.

"Sure thing." She smiled, keying in the addition, and for a fraction of a second, she thought he might be checking her out.

Stupid, stupid, stupid, she scolded herself. *The guy probably has some model wife at home.* She stole a quick glance at his hand but saw no ring on his finger. *Or model girlfriend at home,* she corrected herself.

With her hair pulled back and a silly *Family Burger* hat resting snuggly on her head, she couldn't help but feel a bit self-conscious around this successful entrepreneur. Her shirt, also sporting *Family Burger's* logo, had seen better days.

"That'll be $6.78," she said politely as she snapped back to reality. Of course, he hadn't been checking her out. She scolded herself. The lack of sleep due to school and work was clearly affecting her judgment.

"Thank you," he replied, opening his wallet. In a modest move that didn't go unnoticed by her, he kept it facing himself so as not to flaunt his wealth. Despite this humble effort, she could see him flipping through a number of bills that she could only assume were large denominations. He finally landed on a twenty and handed it to her with a warm smile.

"And what do you do?" he asked with a look of genuine interest. "I mean, aside from working here. What do you do?"

She was a bit surprised by the question and the sincerity in which he asked it. After a brief pause, she answered, "I'm going to school, actually. U of A. Getting a degree in graphic design."

"Oh?" he responded, his eyes widened in fascination. "I have a group of graphic artists working for me at my firm. Are you any good?"

"I've been told I am, but I'm really critical of my work, so it's hard for me to judge," she replied with a shrug.

"Trust me, nobody understands that better than me," he chuckled under his breath.

"This is my fourth and final year, so I'm hoping to get out of this place," she said as she looked around the restaurant.

"Ah, bachelor's degree, I take it?" her suited mystery man asked, once again showing an earnest curiosity in her.

"You got it," she returned without hesitation. "Been a lot of work, but totally worth it."

"You're an interesting young lady..." he trailed off as he leaned in closer to read her name tag, "...Jenna. Pretty name."

"Thank you," she blushed, shyly averting her gaze by staring down at the register.

"I'm Zane. Zane Talbot," he introduced himself with a smile as he extended a big hand towards her, his other still gripping his thick leather wallet. "Nice to meet you."

She returned her eyes to his as she shook his hand, feeling his strong yet gentle touch and hearing herself say the words, "Nice to meet you, too." Her heart fluttered in her chest as his hand engulfed hers, his pale skin contrasting with her dark complexion as their eyes remained locked for a second too long.

"So," he cleared his throat as he shook the moment off, "do you have anything I can see?"

"Any artwork? Not on me, but I have some on my Facebook," she replied while the cooks in the kitchen behind her scrambled to put the order together.

"I'm a bit too busy for Facebook, unfortunately," Zane sighed. "Anywhere else I can go to check out your stuff?"

"Umm..." Jenna began hesitantly. "Well, I did do the artwork on those signs, but it's not very good," she answered timidly as she pointed at the storefront signage.

"You're kidding me?" Zane exclaimed in surprise. "I was checking those out before I came in here. They're awesome!"

"Really?" she replied bashfully with a slight look of embarrassment. "Nah..."

"The burgers, fries, and drinks? Yeah, they're great!" he reassured her as he turned to admire the work once again. Although the back of the signs was facing him, he could still see the art plain as day, thanks to Tucson's bright sun shining through the white paper stock.

"My manager did the lettering. I just drew the pictures," she explained modestly, yet again fidgeting with the corners of the register.

"The pictures steal the show. That's some real talent. Must have taken you hours to do all that, huh?"

The front door's entrance chimed as an elderly man and a boy who appeared to be his grandson strolled into the restaurant.

"Actually, it took me about an hour," Jenna answered, shooting a big smile and friendly wave to the new customers.

"Only one hour? Jesus..." Zane commented in stunned disbelief. "Listen," he began. With a raised finger and a kind smile, he politely gestured for the old man and little boy who'd sidled up next to him to give him another second. "My firm's been looking for a new logo for our company letterhead. My artists are great, but they think a lot alike, and everything they've come up with kind of looks the same. I could really use a new pair of eyes. How about you see what you can come up with, and if I like it, I'll buy it from you?"

"I don't know…" she answered as Zane looked at her almost pleadingly with his captivating eyes. "I don't think I'm good enough for—"

"Nonsense," he interrupted. He reopened his wallet and fished out a business card. "If you hand drew those signs, I have faith that you can do it all. Plus, I'd really like to see some more of your work. My company's always looking for talented artists."

He handed her a business card that she briefly reviewed before shoving it into her back pocket.

"When do you need it by?" she asked as the elderly man and his presumed grandchild stood waiting patiently.

"How's one week sound? I also want to see some of your other stuff. The address and phone number are on the card. Just call my secretary and set up a meeting. Deal?"

"Fair enough," Jenna replied. Zane stepped aside to let the aged man and young boy place their order.

"Order fifty-eight!" a voice sounded from the back. Michael appeared two seconds later with Zane's bag of greasy food and handed it to him with the same friendly smile he'd been trained to deliver. Zane thanked him, and then stood patiently while waiting for Jenna to finish up with her two customers.

"Just wanted to say how lovely it was to meet you, and I look forward to seeing you in one week," he winked, flashing his perfect smile.

"I'll be there, but no guarantees you'll like what I come up with," she sighed as she shook his hand goodbye, her heart once again thudding at his touch and her knees weakening as his blue eyes seemed to peer into her soul.

"Confidence," he said over his shoulder as he made his way toward the door, "is the key to success. One week!"

Chapter Three

Back in the parking lot, Zane found a defeated Carl sitting in the driver's seat with his window down, listening to talk radio. His chauffeur killed the volume at the sight of his approaching boss and leaned out the window to give him the news.

"Tow truck's on the way. The company is sending a new car to get us. Should be here any second."

"Thanks, Carl," Zane nodded as he reached into the bag and pulled out the man's order of fries. As Carl stuffed them down, Zane stood outside the driver's side door, making small talk with him between bites of his burger. It was far too hot to be standing in the sun wearing an all-black suit, but the interior of the limousine wasn't much cooler. Thankfully, the tow truck arrived moments later, and their new set of wheels shortly after that.

By the time Zane arrived back at the office, the *Eegee's* meeting had long since wrapped and Phil Miller had appropriately gathered the art department in the conference room to discuss their new strategy. Not wanting to interrupt their creative process, Zane waited until they'd dispersed before tracking Phil down in the break room to grab the day's highlights. Phil, the chubby marketing whiz who was already balding at only twenty-eight years old, was great at his job despite being somewhat of a loudmouth. He was nothing but professional in front of clients, which was of the utmost importance, but when he wasn't working, he could be overbearingly rambunctious… especially while drinking.

Phil enjoyed his liquor to the point where Zane had to instate a policy barring alcohol from the building after a drunken incident almost costing the firm an arm, a leg, and the reputation they'd worked so hard to achieve. Three years earlier, Phil, having downed a celebratory bottle of vodka after scoring BMW as a client, decided it would be a great idea to slide a hand up his secretary's skirt.

Suffice it to say that it didn't end well, but a lawsuit was avoided after a hefty payout. Understandably furious, Zane had come extremely close to letting Phil go, but his protégé's groveling and tears got the best of him. He decided to keep Phil on board but warned him that such forgiveness would never be seen again. He also docked Phil's pay to reimburse the company for the large check he had to cut the drunkard's former secretary.

Since then, Phil managed to snag the firm another twenty clients while remaining sober, at least in the office, the entire time. His knack for running his mouth, however, hadn't changed, but Zane could overlook that since the guy had made his company a tremendous amount of money over the years. Yes, despite his cocky demeanor and boisterous behavior, there was no denying that Phil was hugely beneficial to the firm. He was terrific with clients, able to lay on the perfect balance of humor and charm, and Zane had entrusted him with the company's largest accounts.

"There's the man!" Phil sounded his familiar greeting as Zane strolled into the break room. "Good job missing the Eegee's meeting."

"Car trouble," Zane shook his head in reply while making his way to the coffee maker.

"I heard. But don't sweat it. The meeting went great. I got it all worked out," Phil boasted with a toothy grin as he sat with his feet resting on one of the break room's circular tables.

"So..." Zane asked, pouring himself a mug of coffee. "Details?"

"We're going to put more of an emphasis on their sandwiches. I convinced them to switch their bread recipe up. We're going to market them as a healthy alternative to fast food. You know, kind of like Subway does," Phil explained before pretending his hands were guns and making his ridiculous "pow, pow" noises.

"A healthy alternative to fast food? Isn't this the place that sells French fries smothered in ranch dressing and topped with bacon?" Zane laughed.

"Yeah, well, we're going to downplay that part," Phil chuckled in return. "And we're going to have them offer fresh cucumber and apple slices as well. You know things like that."

"I like it," Zane smiled as he sat across from Phil. "Slogans? Advertising?"

"Got the art department working on it already, my man," Phil replied confidently.

"Good work," Zane praised, waiting for his coffee to cool down. No cream or sugar for him. He liked it black. He found his mind drifting back to Jenna, the gorgeous young woman he'd met earlier in the day by pure luck. Her long, wavy hair and big, brown eyes were hard to forget, but from the moment he'd laid eyes on her, he'd sensed that she was much more than just stunning good looks. He'd always been good at reading people, and his instincts hadn't failed him regarding this breathtaking beauty. Even though he'd only seen the few drawings decorating *Family Burger's* storefront signage, they'd been enough for him to tell that she was quite the talented artist. He couldn't help but wonder what other surprises this aspiring graphic designer had in store, and he truly hoped to see her again in a week. His thoughts were interrupted by the snapping of Phil's fingers.

"Hey! Hey! Where are you?" he smirked from across the table.

"What? Oh, sorry. Just have a few things on my mind," a flustered Zane replied as he placed the mug to his lips, only to decide the coffee was still too hot. "Listen… I want to revisit the Family Burger account."

"Family Burger?" Phil scoffed incredulously. "Family Burger? Hell, I forgot they were even a client still. Why the fuck would you want to revisit them? Aren't they one of our smaller accounts?"

"I started this company to help businesses succeed," Zane began in his typical matter-of-fact tone. "I drove by one of their restaurants earlier, and they don't exactly look like they're succeeding anymore. I want to fix that."

"Poor management isn't our responsibility, and you know that, man. If I recall, we gave them an awesome campaign they did great with for quite some time. If they're not doing well anymore, it sounds like it's their fault, not ours."

"First of all, *I* gave them an awesome campaign, not *we*," Zane corrected. "Secondly, I don't want to see any business fail." After a moment of thought, he chuckled, "Unless they're our competition, of course."

"Right on," Phil laughed and gave his boss a fist-bump.

"Plus, I forgot how good their food is. Especially for the price."

"Wait, you *ate* there? I thought you said you just drove by," Phil said with his eyes widened in disbelief.

"Okay, okay... I might have grabbed a burger," Zane smirked.

"Zane Talbot, a goddamn billionaire, pulling over to grab a meal at Family Burger," Phil threw his head back and laughed. "I never thought I'd see the day!"

"Whoa, slow down. I'm not a billionaire yet," Zane, grinned. "A few more clients, maybe..."

They shared another laugh, and then went on to discuss the possibility of expansion as Zane casually finished his coffee. With roughly one hundred and twenty clients, yet only fifty overworked employees on the payroll, they'd have to undergo another round of hiring if they wanted to snag more accounts.

Setting up an East Coast branch in New York City and joining the ranks of the Madison Avenue elite weighed heavily on his mind. He'd worked hard to build a successful marketing firm in the Southwest, the most unlikely of places. He knew a location in New York City or Los Angeles was inevitable if he wanted to take business to the next level by forming a corporation. Yes, big changes would have to come soon, and even though he'd only met her briefly, he hoped Jenna would be a part of them.

Chapter Four

"So, who was the suit that was chattin' you up?" Michael asked Jenna after handing order fifty-nine to the elderly man and the young boy accompanying him.

"Said his name was Zane," Jenna answered, grabbing the business card from her back pocket and studying it more thoroughly. "Zane Talbot from Enterprise Marketing. Oh, and he wasn't 'chattin' me up,' you goof."

"Sure looked like it," Michael teased.

"Shut up," she giggled, rolling her eyes. Michael was only one year older than her, and they'd become chummy since he began working at *Family Burger* a year earlier. When he wasn't shouting out order numbers, he was relatively soft-spoken and extremely friendly despite his menacing appearance. One hundred pounds overweight and tattooed-up with a long, thick beard and facial piercings, he was the poster child for never judging a book by its cover.

"What's his story? Not every day we get a suit like that in here," he asked as he looked over her shoulder at the business card.

"I told him I was going to school for graphic art and he asked me to design him a logo," she shrugged while she stuffed the card back in her pocket.

"Think he's legit?" Michael questioned. He headed back to the sink to wash his hands, with Jenna following behind him.

"Didn't you see his limo parked out front?" she replied.

"Gee, I guess I must have missed that. Sorry, the grill doesn't have much of a view," he joked as he reached for a paper towel to dry his hands. Jenna felt silly for asking such a dumb question. Of course, Michael couldn't see the limousine parked out front from his station in the back.

"Well, it was out there. Between that, his suit, and his business cards, I think it's safe to say that, yeah, he's probably legit."

"Rich guys don't typically eat at Family Burger, Jenna," Michael reminded her with a chuckle.

"True, but I'm pretty sure he only came in because his car died. I watched it get towed, then some other car picked him and his driver up a few minutes later," she recounted.

"His driver? How fancy," Michael scoffed, then added, "So, you going to give it a shot?"

"Eh, I don't know," Jenna sighed. "I mean, I want to, but his company looks pretty major, and I'd probably wind up looking stupid. I'm sure he'd look at my designs and laugh."

"Oh, knock it off," Michael snapped back. "If the guy's really on the up and up, you'd be dumb to miss out on such a good opportunity. Aren't you almost done with school? You're going to need a job, and this sounds like a good one."

Conversations like this were why she respected Michael and valued his friendship. She knew he had feelings for her since he'd confessed them to the same coworker who was also her roommate. The news quickly returned to her, but she didn't want to make the workplace uncomfortable or jeopardize their friendship by discussing it with him. He never once made a move on her, never attempted even the slightest flirtation, and always showed her the same level of selflessness that he showed everyone else.

He could have easily dissuaded her from pursuing this opportunity in a selfish ploy to keep her working at *Family Burger* longer, but he simply wasn't wired that way. He truly wanted what was best for her, not what was best for him, and she appreciated that tremendously. Her manager, Juan, was much the same way.

"True," she agreed after some deliberation. "Maybe I'll mess around with a few ideas and see what I can come up with. He wants something by next week. That should be more than enough time."

"Yeah, seriously, especially with how fast you work!" Michael nodded reassuringly. "You got this."

With Michael's confidence boost, she finished her shift and made the short drive home to find her roommate, Leigh, relaxing on the couch with the television on. They'd met and immediately hit it off at *Family Burger* four years prior and had lived together now for almost as long. Leigh's previous roommate had abruptly moved out, and needing somebody to help split the bills, she had invited Jenna to take the open room. Jenna, who had been alternating between her car and a seedy motel, jumped at the opportunity.

They'd remained close despite not seeing each other as often as they used to. Leigh had begun taking evening classes at *Pima Community College* and switched her schedule to work mornings at *Family*

Burger. Their shifts occasionally overlapped, but it was the nights at home relaxing on the couch before bed when the two really got to spend time together. Tonight, however, there would be no time to socialize. Jenna gave Leigh the short version of events while her friend listened attentively, then headed to her room to boot up her computer.

Normally, she'd take a long, hot shower before slipping on her robe and watching television alongside Leigh, but she couldn't get Zane Talbot out of her head. Their entire exchange had lasted only five minutes, yet she'd been thinking about him ever since. His incredible eyes, deep voice, confident stride, perfect smile, firm hands, and commanding presence had completely captivated her. Everything about the man was intriguing and impossible to forget.

With her computer booted and ready to go, she wasted little time heading to Google to search for "Zane Talbot." Her search yielded a plethora of results, all of them impressive.

She found countless articles centered on Talbot himself and his lucrative *Enterprise Marketing*. Nowhere in her search did she uncover anything negative about the man or his company, nor did she unearth any sign of a girlfriend, fiancée, or wife. An image search returned photos of the same gorgeous man she'd met earlier in the day, and the sight of his handsome face made her heart flutter once again. The pictures were mostly of him at company functions or professional shots taken to accompany the articles written about him. Not a single photo showed him with another woman. Jenna found herself relieved by this and quickly chastised herself for it.

Why does it matter if he's with somebody else? A degree and a decent job, Jenna, those are supposed to be your only goals. Besides, like he'd be interested in a girl like you anyway. You work at a goddamn fast food joint.

Years earlier, Jenna had resolved to focus on her education and career, placing them as her highest priority and swearing to remain single until she'd achieved them both. Sadly, she'd seen too many of her high school classmates derail their dreams by falling for the wrong men. She was afraid of making the same mistake and becoming pregnant and alone. In hopes of avoiding this, she decided the best possible prevention was to remain celibate until she had a framed degree on her wall and a reliable, satisfying job.

Yes, at twenty-four years old, Jenna was still a virgin and often struggled with how she felt about that.

Worried she'd be treated differently if people knew the truth, she'd become a pro at changing the subject when it came to sex. She avoided any discussion of her sexual history and, when pressed, would resort to fabricating stories while trying to steer the conversation in another direction.

A year earlier, after downing two big bottles of white wine one night, Leigh had relentlessly grilled her regarding her love life.

"Oh my God, what's the big fucking deal? Just tell me how many guys you've fucked already," Leigh insisted with slurred speech. After twenty minutes of drunken prodding, Jenna finally silenced her with a series of white lies.

"Okay, okay. Four. Now, will you drop it?"

When Leigh demanded more details, Jenna had gone so far as to make up names and stories for all four of her fictional lovers while her friend hung on every word. She didn't blame Leigh for being curious, though. At that point, they'd lived together for three years, and Leigh had never heard Jenna talk about a man, let alone seen her bring one home.

"I actually thought you might be a lesbian," Leigh had giggled before rushing down the hall and into the bathroom to vomit and pass out. Jenna hoped the girl had been too drunk to remember the conversation. Since a year had passed with no mention of it, she could only assume she had.

As the only virgin she knew, she felt like an outcast but remained steadfast in her commitment to her schooling and employment. Still, she did have those moments, incredibly late at night, when the uncertainty of the future kept her awake when she longed for a man's touch. Having somebody by her side, somebody to wrap their arms around her and tell her everything was going to be okay, was something that sounded quite nice indeed.

Somebody like Zane Talbot.

Jenna caught her thoughts drifting to him yet again and scolded herself for the second time that night. She had to keep her eyes on the prize, as she was fond of saying, and that prize was a fruitful career stemming from the hard-earned bachelor's degree that she was only three months short of receiving.

Ignoring the attraction she felt for the man she'd only met briefly, she cleared her head and recognized that a logo design for *Enterprise Marketing* would look damn impressive on a resume. That is if the company chose to use her work. Zane Talbot had proven to be the real deal, which meant it was time for her to get to work.

Opening up Adobe Illustrator, a program she'd grown quite familiar with over the years, she began toying with ideas for the marketing firm's new logo. Zane hadn't given her much to work with, and she was sure that was quite intentional. He'd mentioned that he wanted a pair of new eyes and likely didn't want her to be influenced by his art department's work. She scrapped her first two ideas, believing them too simplistic and amateur, but by her third attempt, an idea was beginning to take shape.

She worked diligently until 2:00 am, then forced herself to get a few hours of sleep. Once she started a project, it was common for her to become so engrossed in it that she'd stay glued to her computer until it was done. She had class first thing in the morning, though, and needed her rest. She backed up her work, pried herself away from her screen, and readied herself for bed. As she drifted off to sleep, thoughts of Zane Talbot's mesmeric blue eyes pervaded her thoughts.

Chapter Five

"Any new messages?" Zane asked Sheryl as he paused in front of his office door. He'd repeatedly asked his secretary this for the last four days, but none of the messages were the one he was hoping for. Jenna still hadn't called to schedule a meeting with him, and he was beginning to think she never would.

"Ali from accounting wants to speak to you about some account discrepancies, and that's it," Sheryl replied apologetically. She clearly knew he was waiting for an important call and could tell by the sunken look on his face that this wasn't it.

"Okay, thanks," he responded politely with a forced smile before heading into his office, shutting the door behind him. With an exasperated sigh, he plopped down into the high-back leather office chair that was seated behind his large, solid oak desk.

His fingers tapped its wooden surface impatiently as he stared down at his work phone and debated calling *Family Burger*. Days had passed, yet he still couldn't shake the image of her big, brown eyes and amazing smile. She looked beautiful, even in her outdated *Family Burger* uniform, and he desperately wanted to see her again. He'd felt an undeniable chemistry with her and was sure the connection was reciprocated. Now, days later, he wasn't as certain of that anymore. His intuition usually never failed him, but it appeared that this time it had. If she hadn't called by now, it probably wasn't going to happen.

The sudden ringing of the same work phone he was staring at startled him so greatly that he almost jumped out of his chair. His adrenaline surged, and his heart raced as he mumbled "Jesus Christ" under his breath. Running one hand through his hair while straightening his tie with the other in an attempt to recompose himself, he inhaled deeply before answering the ringing phone.

"What's up?" he asked informally, knowing it would be his secretary since no calls made it to his desk without passing by her first.

"Mr. Talbot, you have a call from Jenna Parker on line one. Are you available to take it?" Sheryl questioned. She sat only fifteen feet away from him, just outside his office door, but the two agreed that calling worked better than knocking.

"Yes, Sheryl, thank you," Zane answered, trying to contain his excitement.

He left Jenna on hold for a moment so as not to appear too eager and to wrap his mind around the odds of her calling at the same time he'd been thinking of calling her. Seconds earlier, he'd been staring at his phone in deliberation, and by some extraordinary coincidence, perhaps even intervention from above, she was now on the line. The chances of that happening were astronomical, yet it had happened. Perhaps they had a connection after all. He couldn't help but think as he collected himself for the second time. With his calm, confident demeanor back in place, he picked up the phone and pressed the blinking button, signaling line one.

"Jenna, I'm glad you called!" he greeted exuberantly.

"Should I call you Zane, or should I call you Mr. Talbot?" Jenna joked nervously.

"Zane, of course," he chuckled as he leaned forward to rest his arm on his desk. "I'm honestly kind of sick of people calling me Mr. Talbot. Makes me feel old."

"Well, that's because you are," Jenna teased, following it with a giggle that made them both laugh.

"Fair enough. Old man Talbot. Soon, they'll be putting me in a home."

"Oh, shush. How old are you? Thirty-five? You still have a few good years left in you," Jenna fired back.

"That was either a perfect guess, or you've done your homework," Zane replied with a smile.

"You got me," Jenna confessed. "I did a little snooping online to see if I'd be wasting my time on that logo."

"I take it you liked what you saw, then?" Zane asked as he twirled the phone's cord around his finger. He wasn't aware of it, but he had a tendency to do this when he was excited.

"Pretty impressive, I have to admit."

"Why, thank you," Zane responded, genuinely appreciative of the compliment. "So, speaking of the logo… did you get a chance to work on anything yet? I know you're busy with school and work, so I totally understand if you haven't had time yet."

"I actually have them all done and was wondering when a good time to meet with you was. I know you're busy, too."

"Wait, you have them *all* done? What do you mean by *all*?" Zane asked in slight confusion.

"I made a few different versions so you can choose the one you like the best. I mean… if you even like any of them…" Jenna explained guardedly, unsure if she'd made a mistake or not. Zane was quick to assure him that she hadn't.

"Oh, wow, that's awesome! Totally above and beyond. I'm excited to see what you came up with!"

She had the mindset of a true professional, and that fact wasn't lost on Zane. It was routine for him to have his art department offer a client several versions of a logo or advertisement so they could select the one they felt best represented their business. Not only had Jenna done this without instruction, but she'd also done it quickly. He'd given her a week to come up with one logo, yet she'd produced several in only four days.

"When can you squeeze me in?" Jenna asked.

"I'll work around your schedule since mine's probably a bit more flexible," Zane replied understandingly. "When are you free?"

"Amazingly, I have the entire day off Saturday and Sunday, but I figure you're probably out of the office on weekends. After that, my next free time will be… um… let me see," Jenna paused to check her schedule. "Tuesday, any time after 3:00 pm."

"There's no way I can wait until Tuesday," Zane said as he leaned back in his chair. "I'm too impatient. I'm also somewhat of a workaholic and will be here on Saturday," he continued while flipping through his planner.

"Oh? What time can we meet?"

"That's what I'm trying to figure out right now," he answered slowly as he mapped out his day. "How's 4:00 pm sound?"

"That's actually perfect," Jenna replied with a hint of relief in her voice. "It gives me some time to sleep in for once!" she laughed.

"Good. Rest those pretty eyes of yours," Zane dared to say in his first attempt at mild flirtation. Before she could respond, he added, "Oh, and do me a favor and bring in some of your other artwork. I'd love to see as much of it as I can."

"Most of its digital…" Jenna trailed off, hoping Zane would take it from there. He didn't let her down.

"Hell, most of what we do is digital. Throw it all on a flash drive if you have one, and you can show it to me here."

"I can definitely do that, but don't expect anything great. I'm sure I'm nowhere near as good as your art department," Jenna muttered.

"Remember the last thing I said to you when I saw you the other day? Confidence is the key to success. I want you to come in here with your head held high. I have faith in you. Have a little faith in yourself," Zane's commanding voice coached her. "If you're going to make it as an artist, you can't be afraid to show your work."

"Yes, sir," Jenna playfully replied.

"Oh, and give me your number if you'd be so kind. If anything changes, I can give you a ring."

She happily agreed, and he eagerly jotted her digits down in his planner.

"Okay, great! Got it."

"I'll see you Saturday at 4:00 pm, then?" Jenna reconfirmed.

"I'll be here!" Zane replied enthusiastically. "You take care now."

"You too. Bye for now."

"Bye for now," Zane repeated back with a smile as he hung up the phone. He turned his chair to admire the mountainous view out of his office's extensive series of windows. Parker. He now knew her last name, and he'd be seeing her again in two short days. The mere sound of her voice had made his heart melt, and he couldn't remember ever feeling this way about a woman... especially one he'd barely spoken to.

He sensed she had a depth that most beautiful women lacked, and he hoped for the opportunity to explore it. His thoughts were interrupted by the sound of his phone ringing yet again. He quickly swiveled his chair to answer it, excitedly thinking it may be Jenna calling him back.

"Is it Jenna again?" he asked Sheryl, immediately regretting how desperate he sounded.

"What? No," his confused secretary replied. His question had obviously caught her off guard. "It's Ali Chadwick from accounting again. She's out here and says she really needs to speak with you... now."

"Okay, send her in," Zane sighed as he rose from his chair to greet her. He'd hired Ali eight years earlier to manage the books; she'd never asked to meet with him so urgently. He could only assume she needed time off for an emergency of some sort.

His door opened, and he straightened his jacket while Sheryl motioned Ali into the room. He crossed his large office to meet her with a smile and guided her into one of the two chairs seated in front of his desk.

"What can I do for you, Ali? Everything okay?" he asked, returning to his comfortable leather chair.

"Well, that's just the thing," Ali began. She opened the manila folder she'd been carrying and flipped through a few printouts that appeared to be spreadsheets and financial statements. "I've gone over everything a million times, and... it just doesn't make sense."

"What doesn't make sense?" a concerned Zane asked as he rolled his chair closer to his desk and cleared his throat. Ali, a stout, timid girl by nature who was notable for her thick, horned-rimmed glasses, looked especially distraught today. Whatever news she was about to give him was going to be bad, and he knew it.

"I think... I mean... It looks like... I..." Ali stammered.

"Just say it," Zane stopped her. His hands gripped the arm rests of his chair tightly as he braced himself for the news.

"We're missing some money," Ali blurted. She looked as if she were on the verge of tears.

"Whoa, whoa, whoa. What do you mean we're 'missing some money?" Zane asked in frustration while trying not to raise his voice. He prided himself in always remaining calm and collected regardless of the situation.

"Eighty thousand dollars, to be exact," Ali sniffled as she readjusted her glasses. "I don't know how it could have happened. I reviewed our client list again and don't know where it went!"

"First of all, calm down," Zane spoke gently to divert Ali's meltdown. Her cheeks were flushed, her eyes were red, and he could see her hands shaking. "Just relax," he comforted. "Take a deep breath."

His soothing tone seemed to work. Ali relaxed slightly and fumbled with the paperwork she'd been holding.

"Once a year, I sort through our client list and compare how much we budgeted their account with how much we ended up using for their campaign, just like you told me to," Ali began.

"Uh-huh," Zane nodded his understanding.

"Sometimes, we have to go over the budgeted amount, and sometimes, we go under. As you know, everything's documented. When we go over, we note how much we went over. When we go under, that's also noted, and the money's placed back into the marketing account," Ali went on.

"Right," Zane nodded again, gesturing for her to continue.

"We also have the collections account. When a client pays us for our services that money winds up there. That's the same account we use for payroll."

"Yes, I know all this," Zane said in irritation.

"All expenses are documented. Everything. Every cent we spend on a client is accounted for. We keep every receipt, even for a box of staples."

"I know, so how are we missing money?" Zane asked as he placed his elbows on his desk and rested his chin in his hands. He listened attentively as Ali spoke.

"I opened up every client file we have. I've found two clients that..." she paused to find the correct printouts and handed them to Zane. "...don't seem to have any real documentation at all," she finished.

Zane scanned the printouts, reading pieces under his breath as his eyes trailed down them.

"Kroger... forty thousand... Tanque Verde Ranch... forty thousand..."

"See what I mean?" Ali rose from her chair to walk to Zane's side of the desk and read over his shoulder, pointing out bizarre discrepancies in both printouts. "Says we took a total of eighty thousand dollars out of our marketing account to fund their promotional material, but—"

"No expenses are documented," Zane finished her sentence as he nodded his head.

"Exactly. These clients are from eight months ago. It's marked that we completed all of their promotional needs, but there's no expense report and no record of them having ever paid us. The whole thing's just... weird," Ali said while adjusting her horned-rimmed glasses again. She was standing so close that Zane could hear her breathing heavily.

"Let me see their contracts," Zane insisted. Ali rushed back to her manila folder, retrieved them for him, and hurried back to his side.

"I knew you'd want to see them, so I brought them with me," she said with a small smile, clearly pleased at her forethought.

Zane reviewed the two standard-issue contracts, both of them signed, dated, and seemingly in order.

"Basically, we spent eighty thousand dollars to help promote these businesses, we have no record of what we spent that money on, and they never paid us," Zane recapped, baffled by how such a huge financial error could have been made. Sensing the anger under his surface, Ali retreated to her chair and sank into it deeply. Zane could see she was crumbling quickly, once again close to tears, and spoke to her in the same comforting tone he'd used before.

"Look, I'm not pointing any fingers yet. You're not fired if that's what you're thinking." He forced a fake smile, adding, "I'm sure something just slipped through the cracks somehow. We'll find it, and everything will be okay. I bet something just got misplaced."

"O-o-okay," Ali stuttered as she fought back her emotions.

"Head back to accounting, and I'll follow up with this. I'll let you know if I need anything," Zane told her, dismissing her as nicely as he could.

"Okay and… I'm sorry, sir." Ali's voice shook, and the tears welled in her eyes as she left his office with her head hung low.

His door hadn't even finished closing, yet he was already dialing Phil's extension. Seeing that the call was coming from his boss, Phil picked up after only one ring and answered with a typical wise-ass greeting.

"What's up, slut?"

"I need to see you in my office," Zane ordered with a serious voice that Phil fumbled with his words.

"Okay, uh, yeah, okay, be right there."

While he waited for Phil to make the short walk down the hall to his office, Zane closed his eyes and took a deep breath, fully aware of how his mood had changed from good to bad so suddenly. Eighty thousand dollars was an inexcusable amount of money to be misplaced, and it had destroyed the high of speaking to Jenna. He'd been so elated minutes earlier, and now he was fuming mad.

His office door cracked open, and Phil stuck his head in cautiously.

"You wanted to see me?" he asked with concern.

"Come in. Shut the door," Zane instructed in his powerfully deep voice. Phil did as told before, nervously sitting in front of his boss's desk.

"What's going on?" Phil questioned in a hushed tone, his eyes wide and panicked as Zane sat staring at the printouts Ali had given him.

"Take a look at this," he said, sliding the papers across his desk and into his confidant's hands.

"What's is it?" Phil asked as he went over the two printouts.

"That's what you're going to find out for me," Zane replied, folding his hands on his lap.

"Okay?" Phil said slowly, confused by the entire situation.

"We're missing some money. Eighty thousand. I'm sure it's just some clerical error," Zane explained, his mood lightening by Phil's presence. "Looks like we did some work for Kroger and Tanque Verde Ranch and misplaced the expense reports. Can't find any record of them paying us, either."

"Shit. That's no good. I'm sure some chowder head in accounting just forgot to deposit the checks or something," Phil reassured him.

"Well, maybe we shouldn't hire 'chowder heads,' then," Zane, said sternly. "And didn't I leave you in charge of the hiring?"

Realizing he'd inadvertently made himself look bad, Phil swallowed hard and squirmed in his chair.

"No, you're right," he replied apologetically as he began to backpedal, "Everyone in accounting is pretty sharp. I only hire the best. Seriously, I'm sure there's a simple explanation for this."

"My thoughts exactly," Zane nodded. "I'm meeting with an old client today, so I need you to take care of it for me."

"Aye, aye, Cap'n!" Phil rose from his chair and saluted. "I'm on the case!"

"Let me know what you find out," Zane said as Phil approached the door.

"Pow, pow!" was Phil's response. He turned to grin at his boss while pulling the tired move of pretending his hands were guns.

Feeling slightly better about the financial debacle, Zane turned his thoughts back to Jenna in hopes of putting a genuine smile on his face before meeting with his client.

It worked.

Chapter Six

Jenna nervously paced back and forth in her apartment, occasionally glancing in the mirror to reassure herself that she looked presentable. Saturday had come fast, and in a few moments, she'd be leaving to meet with Zane Talbot.

He'd called earlier in the day to confirm their appointment, and the deep sound of his voice had yet again kicked her heart into overdrive. Like the previous two times, their conversation was short, but she hoped that would change today.

She'd been thinking about him all week, despite her best efforts to push him into the inner recesses of her mind, and now she was moments away from seeing the handsome entrepreneur in the flesh. Even more distressing, this charming marketing genius would be judging her work. Her art had always been deeply personal to her, and having it viewed and critiqued was an adjustment she'd had to make when she began taking graphic design classes four years earlier.

She'd learned to let her guard down but found herself panicked by the thought of Zane Talbot reviewing her portfolio. From what she'd read online, he was quite the artist himself, and his designs could be found across the city and the entire nation. He was a prodigy with an inherent understanding of what would please a consumer's eye. Was there any chance her work could possibly please his?

She glanced at the clock for the hundredth time that hour. 3:40 pm. *Enterprise Marketing* was only ten minutes away, but parking downtown could be a nightmare, and she didn't want to be late.

Stealing one last look in the mirror, she grabbed her purse and headed out the door. Climbing into her rusty Ford Tempo, she sat with her hands frozen to the steering wheel as a wave of anxiety rocked her entire body. She was teetering on the edge of a full-blown panic attack when she suddenly remembered Zane's words.

Confidence is the key to success.

With that phrase repeating in her head, she stuck the key in the ignition and thanked her car for starting in what had become somewhat of a tradition over the years. Before kicking her car into gear, she double-checked to make sure the flash drive she'd loaded with her artwork was still in her purse. She mused over how times had changed and how lugging around wallet portfolios had become a relic of the past. These days, a person could fit their entire library of work on a storage device as small as a pinkie finger. A part of her missed the days of carrying a big folder under her arm. It somehow seemed more artistic.

Downtown parking was a pain, as usual, but she finally found a spot and hurried down the sidewalk to the address the business card had given her. It appeared to be a four-story building, and she was surprised to find Zane Talbot waiting for her in the spacious yet rather barren lobby.

He was every bit as handsome as she remembered, perhaps even more so, and he flashed his perfect smile as he moved to greet her with a friendly handshake. He was elegantly dressed in a grey three-piece suit and black tie today, making her suddenly self-conscious about the outfit she'd selected. Given her limited selection, her wardrobe left a bit to be desired, so she'd chosen to wear the only pair of black dress slacks that she owned with a matching pair of black heels.

A black leather belt and a white button-up shirt completed the look, and she accented herself with a series of silver bracelets on her left wrist and a silver chain with a small heart pendant around her neck. Free of *Family Burger* and their policies, she could wear her dark, wavy hair down, and it flowed luxuriously halfway down her backside. A working student who struggled to make ends meet, she couldn't afford to buy a new outfit just for this one meeting. She hoped what she'd gone with would make do.

"Wow," he grinned as their hands locked, sending a shiver of excitement down her spine. His sincere eyes immediately put her at ease as he looked her up and down. "And I thought you looked good before!"

She looked away sheepishly and laughed off his compliment before returning with one of her own.

"As do you," she beamed. "And I did *not* look good before. That stupid uniform… ugh. You have no idea how much I hate it."

"Well, I think you looked adorable," he said as his smile widened, revealing his perfect white teeth. "And I suspect you won't be working there much longer," he winked. "Follow me."

After leading her across the lobby's marble floor to a pair of elevator doors while making idle chit-chat along the way, he hit the fourth-floor button and guided her inside. She used the short ride up to ask him a bit more about his business, trying not to act as nervous as she was.

"So… this entire place is yours?"

"No, no, no," he laughed. "I wish! Maybe someday. Right now, we share the building with three other businesses. We take up the entire fourth floor. The third floor's split between a law firm and a real estate agency. The second floor's a tech support call center, and the ground floor's a paper distributor, which is handy."

"I see," Jenna replied as the elevator chimed and its doors parted, giving way to a large reception area. A plump red-haired woman was seated high behind a tall counter with the words "Enterprise Marketing" decorating its front in big, silver letters. The company's logo, a silver globe with an arrow circling it, was situated to the immediate right of the lettering. It was simple yet beautiful, and Jenna suspected it had been designed by Talbot himself.

The heavyset woman greeted them with a smile and a friendly wave as they passed her. Zane flashed her a polite nod while Jenna returned her wave, and they continued down a long, wide hallway with several doors, some open and some closed, on both sides. Incredible artwork from various marketing campaigns the firm had worked on hung from the walls, and Zane slowed their pace so Jenna could admire it.

"Wow," she gasped, soaking it all in.

"Pretty cool, huh?" Zane grinned as he stole a glance at her eyes that were widened in admiration. One particular piece made her stop in her tracks, and her jaw dropped slightly.

"You did the marketing for Mama's Pizza?" she asked excitedly as she leaned in closer to the framed art.

"Guilty," Zane laughed while looking at her in curious fascination. "I take it you're a fan of that place?"

"Oh my God, yes!" she shot back with uncontainable enthusiasm. "I love it! I go there with my roommate sometimes. Their food is *so* good."

"Ah, so you have a roommate," Zane noted as he stood, taking in her beauty.

"Guilty," Jenna joked while they proceeded down the hallway. She absorbed everything, peeking into the open doors to catch a glimpse of the company's inner workings while Zane happily watched her take it all in. In what appeared to be a conference room, a small group had gathered and seemed to be discussing possible campaign ideas.

In what she instantly recognized as the art department, several men and women were hunched over their drafting tables while others sat in front of computer screens. The room was quite large and brimming with every supply imaginable. Everyone seemed to be working diligently, and when one of the employees spotted Jenna, she shot her a small wave while mouthing the word "hello." Jenna mouthed it back with a smile before resuming her journey down the hallway.

"That's… that's… wow. It's like my dream come true in there," she said in stunned wonderment.

"Not bad, right? That's where most of the magic happens," Zane explained.

The end of the hallway gave way to a shorter, narrower hallway to their right, but they continued straight into the smaller reception area preceding Zane's office. An attractive blonde woman sitting behind a midsized desk stood to shake Jenna's hand as Zane introduced the two.

"Jenna, this is my secretary, Sheryl. Sheryl, this is my friend, Jenna."

The two exchanged pleasantries and shared a moment of small talk before Jenna followed Zane into his office. Jenna didn't miss the gold "Zane Talbot - President" name plate fastened to his door as he politely held it open for her and motioned her into the room. His office didn't fail to impress. The large windows lining the back wall gave way to a beautiful view of the mountains and evoked an exhilarated "oh my" under Jenna's breath. More of his firm's marketing artwork adorned the walls, interrupted by an enormous flat-screen television mounted to her right in the center of the wall. His desk was centered along the back wall just in front of the windows, with what appeared to be a rather expensive black leather chair sitting behind it and two basic office chairs in front of it.

To the right of that sat a low bookcase in the same wood and style as his desk, leading Jenna to believe they were likely part of a set. The bookcase itself was loaded with books, as expected, and the top was lined with framed photos of people she could only assume were friends and family. A black leather sofa was positioned against the wall to her left with a mini-fridge next to it, and a big glass coffee table took up the middle of the room. Potted plants of different varieties sat in all four corners of the office, adding to its overall atmosphere.

With the door shut behind them, Zane made his way to the front of his desk and pulled one of the two chairs out for her. Jenna wasn't sure if he was being professional or chivalrous, but she appreciated the gesture either way. He invited her to sit, and she obliged as he made his way around his desk to sink into his high-back executive chair.

"I'm really glad you made it in today," he smiled. "Would you like something to drink?" he asked as he pointed towards the mini-fridge.

"No, I'm fine, thank you," Jenna smiled back. "And thank you for this opportunity.

"Tell me a little about yourself, Jenna," Zane began, leaning back in his chair and crossing his hands in front of him with his index fingers forming a steeple. "I'd be lying if I said I wasn't curious about you. Are you from around here?"

"New York City, actually," Jenna replied, unsure of what to make of his admission. In what way was he curious about her? "I moved here four years ago."

"From the East Coast to the Southwest. That's quite the change," Zane commented. "Plenty of good schools in the Northeast. What brought you all the way out here, if you don't mind me asking?"

"Oh, you know. Just wanted to get away from the hustle and bustle of the big city. Plus, I have asthma, and everyone always told me the climate out here would help," Jenna, answered, purposely omitting the whole story. She sensed he'd be understanding if she told him the truth about the neighborhood she'd lived in, her dysfunctional family life, and her longing to escape, but opted to keep that to herself for now. She could see in his eyes that he knew she had more to tell, but he tactfully let the topic go with a change of subject.

"What got you interested in graphic design?"

"Well, when I was a kid, drawing was kind of my escape, you know? I used to doodle all the time…" she trailed off, her eyes growing distant as she recalled memories from her previous life. "Mom said I used to draw all over the walls with crayons when I was little. I don't remember doing it because I was so young. One year, I think I was about ten or eleven; she surprised me with a sketchpad and some pencils. God, I was glued to that damn sketchpad. My doodles kind of evolved over time."

"And the graphic art?" Zane asked with a look of sincere interest. He seemed to be glued to her every word, which Jenna wasn't used to but liked.

"Ah, yes. Tablets became all the rage around the time I was in high school, so my grandmother bought me a generic one for Christmas my junior year. Honestly, I didn't even care about the thing until I found out I could draw on it. Being able to erase my work without leaving smudges was one of the biggest appeals," she laughed. "I tend to make a lot of mistakes."

The second those last few words escaped her; she regretted having said them and silently scolded herself for it.

Stupid! Why did you tell him you made a lot of mistakes? Do you ever want a job? Good going, idiot.

"Ha! I know all about that." Zane's hearty laugh interrupted the internal lashing she'd been giving herself. "I'm the master of fuck-ups, to be perfectly blunt. Please excuse my language, but it's true. I'm constantly screwing things up."

His deep laughter was infectious, and Jenna laughed along with him. This gorgeous, powerful man, whose talent had earned him every penny he'd ever made, always seemed to know how to put her at ease. She realized she needed to stop overthinking everything, or she'd end up getting in her own way.

"That makes me feel better," she smiled, adding, "and you don't seem like the kind of guy who ever fu—" she stopped herself short and finished with, "screws up."

"I hate to shatter the illusion, but I'm not perfect. Shhh… don't tell anybody," Zane joked.

"Your secret's safe with me," Jenna giggled.

"Anyhow, let's get down to brass tacks here, shall we?" He pulled his chair closer and folded his hands on his desk. "Let's see those logo ideas. I've been dying to see you all—" he caught his slip and corrected himself with a smile, "been dying to see your work all week."

"Sure, I brought the logos and a few other things on a flash drive," she blushed as she reached for her purse, trying hard not to over-think his last remark. "Right here," she said, handing it to him nervously while hoping he wouldn't see her hand shaking. She'd been trying hard to play it cool, something that usually came quickly to her, but around this man, she found it next to impossible.

"Why, thank you," he smiled, taking her digital portfolio over to the giant wall-mounted television and slipping the device into its USB drive.

"Fancy," Jenna commented as she rose from her seat to stand beside him. Her heart was pounding in her chest, but it wasn't because of Zane's chiseled good looks and commanding presence this time. She was able to distance herself from how attractive he was long enough to view the situation from a pragmatic standpoint. This man was the head of a successful, established company that relied heavily on graphic design. If he liked her work, he'd make an unbeatable reference when it came time for her to find a job in the design field. With only a few months of schooling left, that time was coming fast.

"Modern technology," Zane mused, lifting the remote from the glass coffee table and flipping the television on. Fumbling through the menus, he muttered what sounded like a chain of obscenities as he tried to navigate his way to the flash drive's contents. "You nervous yet?" he joked as he cruised through the sea of menus.

"Very," Jenna chuckled and felt her anxiety fading.

"Seriously, what's the worst that could happen? I hate it so much that I get sick to my stomach, puke all over the floor, kick you out of the building, and tell everyone not to hire you?" he teased with a big grin.

"Shut up!" Jenna giggled, playfully punching him in the arm. He giggled, too, a sound she never expected to hear from a man of such stature, and her face lit up with a smile. Zane's much-needed levity had wiped entirely away her nervousness in a matter of seconds.

"Ah, here we go. Got it," he announced as he looked at the list of file names displayed on the television. "I take it I should start with EMlogo001?" he asked.

"That's right," Jenna replied, still a bit taken aback by how quickly Zane had calmed her.

"I have to say, I'm already impressed just by how you name your files," Zane remarked. "Very organized."

"Thanks. I'm a tad OCD about that," she confessed.

"And… action!" Zane trumpeted as he opened the file.

Jenna turned to gauge his reaction and immediately felt like a weight had been lifted from her chest. A giant smile had crossed his face, and his eyes had come alive excitedly. She let out the breath she'd been holding, relieved by his response. She could tell it was genuine and not forced out of politeness.

"Wow," Zane blurted after his stunned pause. "Wow, wow, wow."

"Yeah?" Jenna asked optimistically.

"Hell yeah!" he returned loudly. "I love it!" He clapped his hands together in amusement as he admired the logo she'd created. A three-dimensional E tilted twenty degrees to the left with an M attached to it. This had been her favorite of the bunch, and she'd appropriately labeled it so it would be the first one he viewed. She hoped the others wouldn't disappoint him.

"You're just being nice," she blushed, even though the look on his face indicated he wasn't.

"No, this is some truly great work," he assured her with a nod. "I'd actually been envisioning something quite similar."

"Really?" Jenna asked with an eyebrow raised skeptically.

"Oh, for sure. The 3D thing's really gotten popular over the last few years. I like it, but only when it's done right... like this," he beamed as he pointed at the screen.

"You know there's more, right?" Jenna smirked, brimming proudly from the injection of confidence he'd given her.

"Yes, let's see what else you've got," he agreed, using the remote to skip to the next image.

For fifteen minutes, he reviewed her work, loving it all and listening as she explained her thought process behind each piece. He occasionally sprinkled in his feedback and suggestions, and they went on to discuss the various programs she'd used to create each image. She explained that she couldn't afford any high-end software as a broke university student. She admitted that a friend had scored her a pirated version of an outdated Photoshop until she could afford to buy a newer, legitimate copy.

Zane didn't judge her for it and actually related to her situation by confessing that he'd gotten his start the same way. The University had provided her with a few decent programs, she continued, but she primarily used cheap or free programs on her home computer to make her visions come to life. Zane was thoroughly impressed by how resourceful she was and by the art she'd been able to produce with mediocre means.

"Well, it's settled," he said as he quickly returned to his desk and sank into his leather chair. She watched as he opened a desk drawer and thumbed through a few papers until he found what he was looking for. He took out a single sheet and placed it on his desk.

He grabbed what appeared to be a rather fancy pen from his jacket pocket and, in one fluid motion, scrawled two lines at the bottom of the sheet in black ink. She couldn't decipher exactly what he'd written from her distance, nor could she make out what he was writing as he jotted on a smaller, rectangular slip that he then stuffed into a white envelope. He attached both the envelope and the sheet of paper to a clipboard he retrieved from the center drawer of his desk before returning to her side by the television. "For you," he smiled warmly as he handed it to her, losing her once again in his baby blue eyes.

"What's this?" she asked curiously while glancing down at the clipboard. The white envelope was clipped in front of what looked like some sort of contract he'd signed and dated at the bottom.

"I love all your work, and your logos were fantastic. That first one, though… You knocked it out of the park. I told you if I chose your logo, I'd buy it off of you, and

I'm a man of my word," his smile widened. "Open the envelope first."

"Okay," she replied slowly as she took the envelope from the clipboard and removed the slip from within it. "Holy shit," she gasped, her mouth falling open in disbelief. It was a check for a staggering three thousand dollars.

"For the logo. If you think that's fair, just sign the release form, and it's yours," Zane told her with a hopeful look.

"This… this… is… way too much," she stammered in bewilderment. "I couldn't possibly… I mean…"

"Nonsense. You did some amazing work, and you deserve every penny," he assured her with a nod.

"I don't know what to say," Jenna blushed, still trying to wrap her mind around the enormity of the check she was holding. "I just feel like this is way too much for those logos."

"No, no, no. Not *logos*," he corrected, "*logo*. Just the first one."

"Wait, you're telling me this," she held up the check for emphasis, "is for that *one* logo?"

"Of course," Zane chuckled. "If you don't think that's fair, we can negot—"

"No, it's more than fair," Jenna interrupted him. "Thank you!" she gushed, an overwhelming sense of pride surging through her.

"Just sign and date this release form right here," Zane said as he moved closer to her and used his elegant gold pen to point to the required lines, "and it's a done deal."

This was the closest he'd been to her yet, and she found his scent intoxicating. She froze for a second, her body paralyzed by their pheromonal exchange while he hovered just over her shoulder. She wasn't sure if he sensed their chemistry as well or if her mind was merely playing tricks on her. She snapped out of her daze and used the pen, engraved with his company's name, to sign and date the form.

"And you're not just being nice?" she blurted as she turned to hand him the clipboard and pen. He laughed at her incredulity as he set the clipboard on his desk and returned the pen to his jacket pocket.

"You overthink too much, don't you?" he joked.

Yes, yes, I do, she thought. *This guy knows me already.*

"It's just that you have this whole team of amazing artists, yet you're going with my logo. Me. A nobody. An outside source with no experience," she replied, expressing her concern.

"Half my team I hired fresh out of school, and most of them went for an associate's degree, not a bachelor's," he explained as he pulled her flash drive from the television's USB port and slipped it into the slim laptop sitting on his desk. "EMlogo001.tcw, I assume?" he asked before transferring the file over.

"Yes, that's right," she nodded.

"And… done!" he announced with a grin. He returned the flash drive to her, and she placed it safely back in her purse. "Now, let's head down to the art department so I can show you the logos they came up with. Maybe then you'll understand why I chose yours."

"You don't have to do—"

She was cut off by the sound of a knock on Zane's door. It cracked open, and a short, pudgy man stuck his balding head in.

"Knock, knock!" he smiled as he casually entered the office with an unsettling grin. Jenna could hear a low groan escape Zane as the man approached them. "I heard there was a hottie in the building, and it looks like it's true," the man said while extending his hand to Jenna, looking her up and down salaciously.

"Jenna, meet Phil Miller," a visibly irritated Zane introduced the two while shooting Phil daggers with his eyes.

"Nice to meet you," Jenna said, forcing a smile as she shook the man's hand.

"And nice to meet you too, m'lady," he replied, lifting her hand and kissing the back of it softly. She shot Zane a befuddled look, which he returned with one of apologetic embarrassment.

"Phil, what have I told you about knocking?" he asked sternly.

"Hey, I knocked!" Phil chuckled.

"What do you want, Phil?" Zane asked in an impatient growl.

"Right," Phil replied, realizing his boss was in no laughing mood and adjusting his demeanor accordingly. "Just wanted to let you know I'm on top of those two accounts we discussed the other day."

"And you had to interrupt my meeting for that?"

"Sorry, I just know it's important and thought you'd appreciate a quick update," he said, his hands working overtime in gesticulation.

Jenna watched the exchange, analyzing the dynamic of the two. She was quick to surmise that, while they were chummy in the workplace, this Phil character tended to get on Zane's nerves.

"Okay," Zane sighed. "Thank you. We'll discuss it later."

He was in the middle of ushering Phil out of his office when his cell phone sounded from his jacket pocket. An intuitive girl, Jenna could sense his agitation growing, although he remained calm on the exterior.

"Just a moment," he sighed after checking to see who was calling. He held up his index finger to indicate it would only take a minute. Phil took it as a signal to stay as well and lingered while Zane shuffled into the corner to take the call.

"Take your time," Jenna smiled politely, pretending not to notice how Phil had sidled up next to her again.

"So, how do you know Zane?" he asked in an attempt to start a dialogue between them. She kept her replies short while her attention remained locked on Zane. His office was roomy, but it was hard not to overhear his call.

"Right now? Mmhmm. Okay. Yeah. Have you tried Kimberly? Okay. Yeah. Mmhmm. No, no, I understand. It's okay. Calm down. I'll handle it. Yeah. Okay. I'll call you then. Bye."

He placed his phone back in his jacket pocket and hurried to his desk, where he pulled a set of car keys from the top drawer.

"Listen, I hate to do this, but I need to run," he sighed, looking at Jenna apologetically.

"Everything okay?" she asked in concern. Since the call had come through on his cell and not his office phone, she figured it wasn't anything related to business. She was right.

"I have to pick my niece up from daycare," he explained as he glanced at his watch.

"Aw, you have a niece? How cute," Jenna smiled. Phil opened his mouth to chime in, but Zane beat him to it.

"Indeed, and she's adorable," he beamed proudly. "Her sitter was supposed to pick her up today. Her pregnant sitter. Her pregnant sitter who just went into labor."

"Yikes," Jenna sympathized, her face a mix of understanding and admiration for this incredible man willing to drop everything at a moment's notice to put family first.

"Rain check on me showing you around the art department?" he asked as he made his way toward his office door.

"Sure," she smiled, her face lit with delight.

"I can show her around the floor right now," Phil blurted eagerly. "I'm between clients and have some time to kill. It'd be my pleasure, really," he continued, pleadingly looking at them. Zane paused to look at Jenna, his eyes tacitly asking her if she was comfortable with the idea.

"Um, sure, why not?" she agreed with a shrug. Phil hadn't made a great first impression, but she was curious to see more of the marketing firm and was willing to give Zane's portly right-hand man another chance.

"Okay, then," Zane forced a smile. "The daycare's on the other side of town, so I won't return for a while. You'll probably be gone by then, so I'll give you a call soon."

As he shook her hand goodbye, their eyes locked onto each other in a silent dance, and she felt the undeniable spark between them. He felt it, too, and this time, she didn't bother questioning it.

"You better," she jokingly demanded with a flirtatious smile. His approval of her work had given her a new-found confidence around him that she'd lacked before.

"Well, okay then," he chuckled, his forced smile now turning genuine. She watched him leave as Phil once again stepped closer to her.

"Ready for the grand tour, m'lady?" he asked with a grin, placing a hand on the small of her back to guide her out of the room.

"Yes, thank you."

Uncomfortable with his touch, she turned her body while she thanked him for breaking free from his intrusive hand.

"So," he started, seemingly oblivious to her sly maneuver, "how did you say you know Zane?"

"He contracted me to do a bit of design work for him," she answered succinctly as she followed him out of the office. He winked at Zane's secretary as he passed her, and she returned it with a poorly-veiled look of disgust.

"Interesting," he replied while they headed down the long, broad hallway. "I've never seen him outsource work before."

"Well, he did," Jenna said flatly.

Phil gave Jenna a detailed tour of the art department, introducing her to the staff and showing her the tools used to bring their marketing campaigns to life. She appreciated him walking her around the room but didn't appreciate how he clung to her side or the flirtatious looks he flashed her.

He swung her by accounting next, then copy, while talking her ear off the entire time. Unfazed by her terseness, he relentlessly boasted about his importance to the firm, referring to himself as the glue that held the place together and the backbone of the entire company. She found him insufferable and didn't know how a man like Zane Talbot could put up with him.

"I really need to get going," she lied as she checked the time on her cell phone. "I'm meeting a friend for dinner soon."

"Just one more thing, I promise!" he insisted, guiding her down the shorter, narrower hallway that she and Zane had passed earlier on the way to his presidential office. It led to a third reception area, this one far smaller than the others, where a beautiful, busty brunette woman sat filing her nails behind a desk that looked uncomfortably small.

"Sharron," Phil paused to greet her. When she dismissively grunted hello without looking up, Phil continued on to the door just beyond her. "My office," he glowed as he motioned Jenna inside and shut the door behind them.

"It's… nice," she placated him while looking around the cramped room. It was a fraction of the size of Zane's office was and looked more like a glorified closet. She couldn't imagine what he could possibly want to show her in here.

"This is where I make this place the money," he smiled proudly.

"That's great," she replied unenthusiastically. Her patience was exhausted, and Phil was killing the good mood Zane had put her in.

"I know it's nothing fancy, but I'll be getting a much larger office when we switch locations," he declared.

"Cool," was her only response as she glanced at her cell phone again, hoping he'd take the hint.

"We should go out sometime," he blurted unexpectedly, completely catching her off guard.

"Excuse me?" she asked in shock, a slight chuckle of disbelief escaping her.

"Me and you. We should go out sometime," he repeated with a goofy grin that she assumed was supposed to be seductive.

"Look, I don't think—"

"Ah, taking the hard-to-get approach," he interrupted her. "I like that," he added with a smirk as he moved in closer to her.

"Okay, I need to go now," she said in a panic, the urban dialect she'd worked hard to lose rising to the surface again.

"Oh, come on," he replied with an exaggerated pouty face. "I have a lot to offer, you know."

Her heart thudded in her chest, but it wasn't due to attraction like it was with Zane. This man was giving her the creeps, and she wanted out by any means possible. He had her up against the door, and her hands worked feverishly behind her back to find the doorknob. He now stood so close that she could feel his breath on her skin. To avoid a potential scene, she told him what he wanted to hear.

"O-o-okay," she stammered with a big, fake smile. "I have the firm's number. I'll call you."

"That's my girl," he grinned, then touched his thumb and index finger to her chin. "You truly are beautiful."

"Thank you," she managed to spit out as she swallowed hard. She slipped out the door and hurried out of the building as quickly as possible.

Chapter Seven

She'd just thanked her car for starting when her cell phone rang. She was still reeling from Phil's disturbing behavior, and her heart began pounding again at the thought of the call possibly being from him. She didn't recognize the number but knew she hadn't given Phil hers and that if he did manage to find it, it likely wouldn't be this fast. Curiosity got the better of her, and she answered cautiously.

"…Hello?"

"Hey, Jenna, Zane Talbot again."

She sank into her seat with a sigh, all tension instantly relieved by the sound of his voice.

"Hey, you," she chirped, her spirits lifted once again. "I almost didn't answer 'cause I didn't recognize the number."

"I'm calling you from my cell instead of my work phone. Feel free to save this number. It'll be the best way for you to reach me."

She found herself wondering if he had given everyone his personal number or if he'd made an exception for her and reminded herself not to overthink such a trivial thing.

"Okay, will do."

"I just wanted to give you a quick ring to apologize for having to duck out so quickly."

"Oh, I completely understand, so don't even worry about it," she assured him.

"Did Phil give you the grand tour?" he asked. From the focused tone of his voice and background noise, she could tell he was driving.

"He sure did," Jenna replied flatly.

"How'd it go?"

"It was… interesting," she told him with ambivalence, debating whether or not to mention Phil's inappropriate flirtation. She sat with her car idling, watching pedestrians as they casually strolled by.

"Just interesting? Sounds like you weren't too impressed," Zane remarked with a hint of disappointment.

"No, no, don't get me wrong. I loved it! Your company's amazing, and the art department is… wow. Everyone was so nice. Thank you for letting me see everything," she said pleasantly. Jenna opted to put the Phil incident behind her, for now, to avoid causing any waves. She had a good thing going with Zane and didn't want anything messing it up.

"You're quite welcome," he responded, sounding relieved to hear that his firm didn't disappoint. "Listen, there's a reason I'm calling…"

"Yes?" she asked while a barrage of possibilities ran through her mind.

"You told me you have Saturdays off, right?"

"Yes, that's right," she replied slowly, hoping wherever this was going led to seeing his handsome face again.

"I have a few things I'd really love to talk to you about. What are your plans for tonight?" he asked optimistically.

"I don't have any," she answered excitedly.

"Well, you do now," he laughed. "I want to discuss a few things over dinner."

"You're… asking me to dinner?"

"That's right, and I won't take no for an answer," he insisted.

"Well, gee, I guess if you bend my arm," she replied coolly, trying her best to mask her excitement.

"How's 8:00 p.m. work for you?"

According to the clock on her car's outdated stereo, it was already 5:30 p.m. That didn't leave her much time to prepare, and with her credit union being closed, she couldn't deposit the generous check he'd cut her. She certainly didn't have enough money left in her account to run out and buy a new outfit, nor did she have the time if she wanted to be ready by 8:00 p.m. She'd have to rummage through her closet in hopes of finding something presentable enough for whatever he had in mind.

"Um, sure, that works just fine," she lied as she put her car into gear and pulled away from the curb. She had no time to spare if she would make this work. "What were you thinking?"

"I was hoping I could take you to my favorite restaurant. Do you like Italian?"

"I do," she answered, heading back to her apartment complex, "and that sounds wonderful. What's the restaurant?"

"Jesus, this idiot almost hit me," he grumbled in irritation. She heard a car horn in the background, indicating he'd just come dangerously close to a collision of some sort. "How about you text me your address, and I'll pick you up at eight sharp, good?"

She decided against repeating her question. She'd hoped for at least some indication of where he'd be taking her but had to admit that the surprise was somewhat of a thrill. Wherever it was, she knew it would likely be fancy and require something formal. She was already going through her wardrobe in her mind, frantically trying to figure something out.

"Okay, I'll text you as soon as I get home," she assured him. With a quick exchange of goodbyes, she continued darting in and out of traffic in an attempt to get home as fast as possible. Time was ticking.

She was relieved to see that Leigh's car wasn't in the parking lot of their complex. This meant she wasn't home and that she didn't have to burn precious time recounting her eventful day. She loved the girl, but Leigh could be a stickler for details, and 8:00 p.m. would be here before she knew it.

She rushed upstairs to their second-story apartment, barreling through the front door and throwing her purse on the couch as she quickly headed to her bedroom. She paused to pull her cell phone from her pocket and sent Zane her address. He replied moments later with, "Great, see you then!"

After ten minutes of tearing through her closet, she settled on a black evening gown she hadn't worn since high school and hoped it would be classy enough for wherever they were going. She carefully selected a pair of white gold earrings, which triggered the painful memory of having to pawn the necklace her grandmother had given her.

When she'd pawned it four years earlier, she'd planned on using her first paycheck to get it out of hock, but that hadn't exactly worked out. She'd been overcome by bills, and by the time she had enough saved up to buy the necklace back, it had already been sold. It would have matched the earrings perfectly, she lamented as she searched for another necklace that would suffice.

She decided to go with the heart pendant she was already wearing. It had become her favorite, and although it was sterling silver, it matched the earrings closely enough. Under scrutiny, it would be obvious that the pieces didn't come from the same set, but she didn't think anybody would notice at a glance.

In the bathroom, she stripped naked and posed in the mirror as the shower heated up behind her. She'd been working at *Family Burger* for four years now, and with their food being so cheap, it was often her only option. She turned to the side and sucked in her stomach to assess how much weight she'd put on since she'd been hired. The dreaded scale had told her five pounds when she'd weighed herself a month earlier, and she didn't think that was so bad considering she'd been slinging fast food for so long. She lacked the funds or the time to join a gym but would occasionally pop in Leigh's *Zumba at Home* DVD for a quick workout.

Suddenly aware of how conscious she was being about her weight, Jenna realized that, once again, she was reading too much into things. She didn't even know if Zane's dinner invitation was romantic or professional.

Given the chemistry between them, she'd inferred that it was more romantic than platonic. Despite the good looks everyone claimed she had, she'd never been too smooth with men. She did know enough to tell when she was being hit on, as the guys in her old Brooklyn neighborhood weren't exactly subtle in their approach. She'd grown quite used to the wolf whistles and inappropriate comments that peppered her walk home from school every weekday or on the short trek to and from the local market. In her new Southwestern life, the men were a bit more tactful, yet their intentions were still easy to read. Regardless of where they were from or the strategy they used, their end game always seemed to be the same. None of these men cared about her mind; they just wanted her body. Because of this, she was quite selective in who she shared her time with.

To help herself feel normal, she'd ventured out on a handful of dates over the years, but none of them had extended beyond making out and light petting. She'd never met anybody who made her heart race like Zane Talbot. Just thinking about him made her giddy, and that was a feeling she'd never experienced before.

Jumping in the shower, Jenna thanked herself for having shaved her legs that morning and not wasting valuable time with that daunting task. She quickly rinsed off while recalling how surreal the last two hours of her life had been.

Zane had loved her work and paid her liberally for it, and they seemed to have forged a connection of some sort. She caught a glimpse of his company's inner workings, and his right-hand man had creeped her out by coming on way too strong. Zane had asked her out, his motives unclear, and now she was hurrying to get ready for dinner at an undisclosed location.

She could never have predicted this day, and it wasn't over yet. Nervous for the evening and praying she wouldn't make a complete fool of herself, she leaned her back against the shower wall, hoping the warm water would help calm her anxiety. No man had ever come close to affecting her like this.

Toweling off, she let her hair air dry as she carefully applied a faint spattering of gold shadow across her eyelids, hoping Zane would like the choice. Even if the dinner was business and nothing more, she hadn't gone out in months, aside from a trip to the local pizza joint here and there with Leigh, and wanted to look her best. She refocused her efforts, paying meticulous attention to every detail as she finished applying her make-up.

When she was satisfied with her job, she headed to the small living room, where she flipped on the television and plopped down on the sofa. She meticulously painted her fingers and toenails the same dark red as her lipstick, paying Dr. Phil only half of her attention. As her nails dried, she reached for the remote and changed the channel carefully so as not to mar the tacky paint.

"What a quack," she commented under her breath as she searched for something a bit more appealing. She tried to focus on a celebrity cooking show, but her mind couldn't stop drifting to thoughts of Zane Talbot. She couldn't imagine what business he'd possibly have to discuss since the logo work he'd requested was now a done deal. He did know she was graduating soon, and since he seemed to genuinely like her work, there was always a chance he might offer her a job.

While it was confirmed that she would be looking for a full-time design position soon, the thought of the dinner being romantic excited her more than anything. She scolded herself for putting lust before career and glanced at the clock for the umpteenth time.

The minutes ticked by until 7:30 finally hit, and with a half-hour left to get ready, she headed to her bedroom to slip into the black evening gown she'd laid out on her bed. She slid her feet into the black stilettos she'd chosen and twirled in front of the full-length mirror mounted to the back of her door. From there, she hit the bathroom again to fix her hair and apply a few slight touch-ups to her make-up. Normally a very modest girl, she had to admit she looked good.

As she admired herself, she realized just how much she enjoyed getting dolled up to go out. She'd never put this much time into herself, mostly because her previous dates weren't worth the effort. They were with good men, but none of them made her heart flutter like Zane Talbot did.

With the sun down and the desert heat had subsided slightly, she stood on her small balcony and took in the silhouette of the mountains while casting glances down at the parking lot below. She wasn't sure what Zane would be driving or if he'd even be driving since he was being chauffeured in a limousine when she'd first seen him only days earlier. Two minutes before 8:00 p.m., a black town car slowly rolled into the lot beneath her. The manner in which it crept indicated that the driver was attempting to find the right address. Although it was getting dark, she could see Zane Talbot, dressed to the nines as usual, step out of the back to survey the complex.

"Hey, you!" she shouted down at him, ending his confusion.

"Hey!" he smiled up at her as he walked closer to her balcony. "These damn buildings all look the same," he laughed.

"Oh, I know," she replied as she smiled back at him, "but I'm glad you managed to find it."

"Can I come up?" he asked his striking good looks and captivating charm impossible to turn down.

"Sure, the stairs are right there," she told him as she pointed around the corner.

"On my way!"

Showtime, Jenna said to herself as she watched him disappear around the side of her building. A few seconds later came a gentle rapping on her door. Trying not to appear too eager, she paused momentarily and took a deep breath before opening it as nonchalantly as possible. She greeted Zane with a friendly smile.

"Right on time," she noted.

"Wow," he gasped, as he looked her up and down with his mouth agape. "You look absolutely stunning."

"Thank you," she blushed. "You look nice, too."

"I mean, just... wow," he reiterated. "Now I feel underdressed."

He'd changed from his grey three-piece suit into a black one and looked strikingly dapper as usual. Jenna wondered if he even knew how to dress casually.

"Oh, shut up, you look fine," she replied playfully while rolling her eyes. "Let me just grab my purse, and we can get out of here."

"So, this is where you live, eh?" he asked curiously as he peeked inside without being overly intrusive.

"Yes, this is my palace," she joked, quickly grabbing her black clutch from the kitchen counter. "Try not to be too jealous."

She couldn't help but notice that he had politely remained outside and hadn't made any attempt to invite himself in. She respected that, and with her clutch in hand, she headed out the door, stopping to lock it behind her.

"It's not a bad place," Zane said, resuming the conversation as they headed downstairs. "Looks cozy from what I saw."

Reaching the parking lot, he hurried ahead to open the waiting town car's back door for her.

"Thank you," she said, acknowledging his chivalry with a polite smile as she comfortably situated herself in the vehicle's back seat. Seeing that she was settled in, he shut her door and walked around the car to sit next to her.

"See? I don't always ride in a limousine," he said humorously.

"Yeah, but you still have a driver," she ribbed while rolling her big, brown eyes as the car set off toward the undisclosed destination.

"The limousine's mostly to impress clients," he divulged. "Shh... don't tell anyone," he winked as he placed his index finger to his lips.

"And the driver?"

"Mostly for meetings," he explained with a smile. "And I do a fair amount of my own driving, I'll have you know."

"Oh, so this is a meeting?" she smirked, looking into his gorgeous blue eyes.

"No," he returned her gaze intently, "I just wanted to give you my fullest attention tonight. No distractions. I want to focus on you for every second I have you," he grinned.

"Oh?" Jenna gulped a sudden wave of heat coursing through her. The energy between them was palpable, and she suddenly had no doubt that this outing was much more than business.

They rode for fifteen minutes, with conversation flowing freely along the way. Despite her initial burst of nerves, she found herself quickly at ease in his presence. Her confidence, which had never been shaken by a man before, had now returned. Laughter radiated from the back seat as they playfully bantered, enjoying each other's company as the town car weaved through the city.

Arriving at the restaurant, Jenna wasn't surprised to find it was one she'd never heard of before. As a transplant from New York City and a broke one at that, she'd never experienced Tucson's fine dining and rarely ventured into the business district.

Zane helped her out of the car and guided her inside, where her senses were immediately overcome with Italy's sights, smells, and sounds. As she would quickly find out, *Primavera* was a five-star restaurant known for its wealthy clientele. It was where the city's social elite gathered to feast on authentic Italian cuisine, and its lavish interior was unlike anything she'd ever seen.

The decor was immaculate; its stone walls adorned with artwork she knew was expensive. The lighting was low, adding an almost romantic ambiance throughout the restaurant, and Sicilian music played softly in the background.

She went from a sense of welcome to a feeling of dread as she surveyed the mobbed dining area located to the left of an impressive full bar. The city's most prominent businessmen and women sat feasting on *Primavera's* pricey courses, all of them dressed to the hilt. She glanced down at her dress, suddenly self-conscious in her choice of attire, and she could feel her face grow flushed as the hostess approached them.

"Zane Talbot, reservation for two," Jenna heard him tell the woman as she continued absorbing the restaurant's atmosphere. She knew New York City must have restaurants as nice as this, but she'd never had a chance to experience any of them.

"You look gorgeous," he whispered to her as the hostess guided them to a private table in the far corner of the dining room. He'd sensed her concern, and the sincerity in his reassuring words instantly soothed her. She followed closely by his side as they crossed the busy floor.

"Thank you," she whispered back, unsure if Zane could even hear her over the low roar filling the restaurant.

Seating them at their table, the hostess pleasantly informed them that their waiter would be with them shortly before returning to her station by the restaurant's entrance. Jenna was left sitting at a candlelit table across from a rich, handsome man she hardly knew but was undeniably attracted to.

"What do you think?" Zane asked eagerly while studying Jenna's face for a reaction.

"This is too much," she replied with an awestruck smile, continuing to soak in the restaurant's decor. Their table was slightly recessed from the rest of the room, and she felt he'd paid a lot of money to have it arranged that way. It was draped with a white tablecloth, and a small floral arrangement sat beside a tall, red candle. Although she couldn't smell them over the restaurant's savory aroma, she could tell the flowers were real.

"I seriously can't get over how beautiful you look," he grinned as he looked her over.

"I'm so underdressed," she said with a quiet nervousness. "I feel like everybody's looking at me."

"Oh, stop." His smile widened, and his baby blue eyes lit up. "Seriously, you look amazing. Belle of the ball!"

"I'm wearing all black," she commented while looking down at her outfit. "I look like I'm going to a funeral. Why did I wear this? Ugh. Stupid."

"You're ridiculous," Zane teased. He'd placed a hand over his mouth, and his chest heaved as he silently laughed in amusement. "Hey, maybe this date will be the death of you!" he moved his hand to blurt comically.

Jenna couldn't help but giggle. He seemed to have a way of alleviating her anxiety. A few hours earlier, she'd been a nervous, self-conscious wreck around the man, but all of that had somehow changed, stemming from both his approval of her work and the flirtatious suggestion that he found her attractive.

A friendly waiter hurried over to deliver a basket of fresh ciabatta bread and take their drink orders. In a gentlemanly fashion, Zane gestured for her to place her order first and looked at her curiously when she only asked for water.

He ordered a glass of red wine, and as the man hurried off to fetch their drinks, Jenna followed Zane's lead and opened her menu. The selection was wonderful, but she couldn't believe the prices she saw as she scanned the list with wide eyes.

"Do you know what you want?" Zane asked while he scoured his menu as well.

"Jesus, the prices are... And I thought the drinks were..." Jenna mumbled, trailing off as she realized the thoughts she'd been meaning to keep private had unintentionally come tumbling out of her mouth.

"Wait, is that why you only ordered water? Because you're worried about the prices?" Zane questioned, his brow raised in worry.

"Well, come on. A soda is, like, seven bucks—" she started, only to be interrupted by Zane's deep voice.

"You order whatever you want, okay? Don't worry about price. Not tonight."

"Are you sure?" she asked. "I mean, you've already done so much for me today. That check was—"

"You earned that check," he interrupted again, suddenly serious, "and you've earned this dinner. So, please order anything on the menu. I mean it."

"Okay," she conceded apprehensively.

"If it makes you feel any better, I'll write the entire meal off as a tax deduction," he joked, sensing her trepidation.

"Doesn't that only apply to business meetings?" she smiled as she turned her eyes back to the menu. She'd never been to a restaurant where the menus didn't feature pictures of the food. This place was indeed fancy, she noted as she made her choice.

"Well, since you mentioned it, I do have some business I'd like to discuss," he announced, adjusting his posture and folding his hands on the table before him.

"Oh?" she asked with her brow raised in interest. "And what business is that?"

"My unexpected stop at Family Burger made me realize we haven't heard much from them over the last couple of years. They were doing well, then suddenly stopped expanding and halted their advertising campaigns," he explained.

"Go on," Jenna prodded.

"I've been in touch with Paul Lopez over the last few days. He and his wife started the chain together over twenty years ago."

Jenna nodded her understanding, listening attentively as he continued.

"Turns out his wife got sick a few years back. Cancer. They sunk all their money into her treatment."

"So that's why they stopped expanding," Jenna pieced together. "My manager told me she was sick but didn't give me many details."

"Exactly. It crippled them financially. They barely had the money to keep their existing stores open, let alone pay for marketing," Zane replied as the waiter brought them their drinks. Insisting that Jenna enjoy the red wine with him, he asked the man to bring the entire bottle and an additional glass. The waiter darted off to retrieve it as Zane went on.

"They were keeping the severity of her illness fairly hush-hush. She's gone into remission, thankfully, and things are looking good."

"That's a relief," Jenna agreed. Paul Lopez and his beautiful Dominican wife had visited her store several times, and they both seemed like wonderful people. They treated their employees with the utmost respect, even taking the time to learn a little about their personal lives. It made the "Family Burger" title seem much more fitting.

"They want to begin advertising again, but they're still recovering from the huge financial blow," Zane told her. Always the gentleman, he refused to touch his wine until she had hers and waited patiently for their waiter to return.

"So what are you going to do?" Jenna questioned, hanging on his every word.

"I agreed to work with them at half the normal rate. We have a history together, so I figured it's the least I can do."

"Didn't you say they were one of your first clients?" Jenna asked.

"That's right," Zane replied with a small smile, clearly shocked that she'd remembered this detail, "they were. They were willing to give a nobody like me a shot, and I owe them for that."

"That's really sweet of you," Jenna smiled affectionately.

The waiter reappeared with the requested bottle of wine, pouring Jenna a glass and gently placing it in front of her. He set the bottle on the table and politely asked if they were ready to order. Once again, Zane motioned for Jenna to go first, and she stumbled as she attempted to pronounce the penne all'arrabbiata. Zane silently chuckled at how adorable this was, and even she had to giggle at her own fumble. He effortlessly ordered the pollo alla cacciatore, and their waiter departed with a smile.

"Anyhow, this is where you come in," Zane resumed after coaxing Jenna into trying the wine. She'd never been a huge wine drinker, or drinker in general for that matter, and its bitterness caught her off guard.

"How so?" she asked as she forced the sip down.

"I want your help with their campaign," he said bluntly. He took a sip of wine, his eyes locked intently on hers.

"My help? Why? I mean, you have an entire team, and I wouldn't even know where to begin!" Jenna spat, stunned by his proposal.

"You'd be perfect," he persisted. "You've been working with Family Burger for how long? You know their menu and how they operate inside and out."

"Well, that is true," she conceded. "What are you suggesting?"

"I'm not suggesting anything," he smiled as he took another gulp of wine. "I'm telling you flat-out that I want you to join my firm."

"Zane…" she began. "That sounds wonderful, but between school and my job, there's no way I'd have the time for that." She nervously took another sip of wine, which went down much smoother.

"No, no, you don't seem to understand," he countered, leaning closer. "I want you to leave Family Burger and work for me. I know you have school, but we can work around that. It's not a problem."

"Jesus, this is so…"

"Unexpected?" Zane finished for her. "I know, but I'm very impressed with your work, and the Family Burger account would be the perfect campaign to start you out on."

"I don't know…" she replied hesitantly. "This is all so sudden."

"To be honest, I was going to offer you a job when you finished your schooling anyway," Zane admitted. "I might as well bring you on board now, though. No sense in waiting, especially with the Family Burger account opening back up."

The waiter returned, briefly interrupting them to drop off an antipasto salad and two small plates. Zane nodded a thank you at him, and he raced off for the third time. Zane wasted no time returning to his offer.

"You'd be working less hours than you are now and with better pay. Plus, you'd be doing something you love and are amazing at. Seems like a no-brainer to me," he persuaded.

She had to admit that his proposition sounded extremely enticing. She'd planned on searching for new employment in a few months anyhow and definitely wouldn't miss slinging greasy cheeseburgers. Juan, her manager, would be sad to see her go, and Michael would be as well, but they both knew she planned on leaving soon. This opportunity could launch her career and working for Zane's successful firm meant she'd be seeing the gorgeous entrepreneur regularly. As much as she hated to admit it, that alone was incentive enough.

"Okay, you've sold me on this idea," she beamed. "I'll have to talk to my manager and put in my two-week notice."

"Already taken care of," Zane smirked.

"Wait, what?" she asked, puzzled.

"I had a talk with Paul about you after we spoke on the phone earlier. I told him what a talented artist you are and that I'd like you to help with their marketing since you're so familiar with their brand. He agreed it was a great idea and also agreed to let you go without a two-week notice. He just asks that you cover one last shift on Monday. After that, you're all mine."

"Geez, you really thought of everything, huh?" Jenna joked as she picked at the salad. She hadn't eaten anything since the early afternoon and was ravenous but didn't want to fill up before the main course arrived.

"I'm always thinking two steps ahead," Zane said with a devilish grin.

"Well, I hope you're making the right decision here," she gulped, washing her salad down with some more wine. "I don't know much about marketing."

"You'll learn," he assured her. "Besides, the backbone of my company is art."

"Phil said *he's* the backbone of your company," she chuckled.

"Did he really say that?" Zane laughed along with her. "Typical Phil. The guy's kind of a schmuck, but he brings in business somehow."

"He seems quite… assertive," Jenna replied, rolling her eyes.

"That he is," Zane agreed as he finished the rest of his wine.

She was gearing up to ask about his relationship with Phil when he abruptly changed the subject.

"That's a pretty necklace."

"Oh, this?" she blushed as she instinctively touched the silver heart pendant. "Thank you."

"I noticed it back in my office," he added while pouring himself another glass of wine. He politely topped off hers as well.

"Nothing gets by you, does it?" she quipped, taken aback by how observant he was. She hadn't seen him so much as cast a glance at the necklace earlier, and her shirt had done an excellent job concealing it.

"I notice everything. Attention to detail's the main reason I've been successful," he pointed out.

"My grandmother gave me a beautiful diamond necklace when I was sixteen," she told him as her face turned sullen, "before she died. I was so broke when I moved here that I had to pawn it. Worst mistake ever. I would have worn it tonight."

Jenna wasn't sure if his kind eyes or the wine had prompted her to share this. She would have regretted it had he not looked at her with such compassion and understanding.

"I'm really sorry to hear that," he replied sympathetically. "Sounds like you did what you had to do to survive. I'm sure your grandmother would understand."

"She was a great woman," Jenna swallowed as she worked hard to contain her emotions, "and I'd like to think you're right."

"So, who gave you that necklace?" he asked, leaning closer to admire the heart pendant. "Boyfriend?"

"Ha!" she laughed louder than she'd intended to. She was definitely feeling the effects of the wine. "No, I bought this myself at Kohl's for twenty bucks. Pathetic, right?"

"Not pathetic at all," he reassured her with a warm smile. "I'm just fishing for information on your love life."

"Is that so?"

"Yes. I find it hard to believe a woman as enchanting as you are single," he remarked.

"Well, believe it. I've had my share of options," she allowed herself to boast, "but I wanted to put school and career first. No distractions that way."

"Smart," he agreed. "But don't you get lonely?"

"I'm too busy to get lonely," she laughed, omitting the nights she'd wished she had a man to hold her. She turned the question around on him by asking, "What about you? How's a handsome, successful man like you still on the market?"

"Maybe I should do a better job advertising myself," he joked. Jenna chuckled and sipped more of her wine. She was slowly warming up to its taste.

"So, you don't have some wife or girlfriend stashed away somewhere?" she asked as she enjoyed more of the salad.

"Nah. In all seriousness, I've been so focused on building my company that I kind of put dating on the back burner," he explained. "I mean, I've dated here and there over the years, but nothing too serious. I guess I'm like you in that regard. You know, putting my goals first."

"That makes sense," she said and, after a pause, teased, "but you're not getting any younger."

"I know, I know. Now you're sounding like my mother," he laughed.

"I'm sure she's quite proud of you," Jenna smiled.

"She is, but she also wants a grandchild," he shook his head while rolling his blue eyes.

Jenna used this opportunity to ask about his personal life. She'd been itching to know more about him, and this was the perfect chance.

"Do you have any brothers or sisters? Earlier, you said you were picking up your niece, so I assume you do."

His face suddenly grew somber, his demeanor abruptly changing as a deep sadness seemed to overtake him. He took a swig from his glass while avoiding eye contact with her by looking around the room.

"I had a younger brother, yes," he began slowly, "but he passed away."

"I'm so sorry to hear that," Jenna consoled, tears welling in her eyes from the look of pain on his face.

"IED over in Iraq five years ago," he expounded after taking yet another gulp of wine.

"That's terrible," she replied, her hands instinctively covering her heart as she felt the agony of his loss.

"Left me a gorgeous little niece, though," he forced a chuckle in an attempt to lift the mood. "What about you? Brothers? Sisters?"

"I have two brothers. Used to have three," she answered softly, breaking eye contact by looking down at her plate.

"You lost a brother, too?"

"Yes. I didn't exactly live in the best area..." she confessed as she finished her wine. "Gang life doesn't seem to work out for anybody in the long run."

As intuitive as he was handsome, Zane was able to piece the story together from there.

"I see," he nodded understandingly.

"Anyhow, enough about that," she said. She cleared her throat and poured herself one more glass of wine.

"Agreed," he smiled. "I really do want to know all about your life, though. I find you quite fascinating."

"Me?" she giggled, her head beginning to spin from the wine. "Nothing is fascinating about me. I promise you that."

"Oh, I beg to differ. It's not every day I meet a woman who's as talented as she is beautiful."

"Why, thank you," she blushed and returned the flirtation. "And I could say the same. It's not every day I meet a handsome, creative man."

"I'm sure there are plenty of good-looking artists at the University," he said skeptically.

"Eh, guys my age only want one thing," she shrugged.

"True. Us older men are where it's at," he winked with a grin. "But, seriously, tell me more about your life. In my office, you gave me the broad strokes, but I want the fine details."

The combination of wine and his compassionate blue eyes had put her completely at ease. No longer worried about his judgment, she opened up about her childhood and the rough life she'd lived growing up in one of Brooklyn's most notorious neighborhoods.

She paused when their dinner arrived and resumed while they enjoyed the incredible food. She felt like she was rambling, yet the look of interest on his face never waned. When she was done sharing, he reciprocated by opening up about his life as well. His father, hardened from his service in Vietnam, had been a strict disciplinarian with hopes of his sons becoming military men. He'd been disappointed when Zane chose to pursue marketing instead of a military career, and seeing that disappointment led to his brother joining the army, where he was subsequently shipped overseas to fight a questionable war. His father had since passed, and his mother had retired four hours north in Sedona.

They'd never been too close but typically kept in touch once a month via phone. He helped out his brother's widow whenever possible by helping her financially and taking his niece every other weekend to help alleviate some of her burdens. He loved the little girl dearly and cherished every second he spent with her. He beamed with pride as he scrolled through his phone, showing Jenna pictures of the little girl and his departed brother, who he rightfully touted as a hero. Jenna felt honored that he would share such personal photos with her, and her heart throbbed at how his face lit up when he looked at them.

Jenna was stuffed to the gills, but Zane insisted she try a Sicilian cannoli. She agreed under the condition they'd split one and joked that she'd have to work out twice as hard the following week. He silenced any lingering insecurities by complimenting the physique she'd managed to keep after years of working in an establishment that dealt primarily with cheeseburgers. They bounced flirtations off each other while waiting for the bill, and when it arrived, Zane politely thanked the waiter while keeping the total concealed from her. He fished his wallet out of his back pocket and discreetly placed a single green note inside the check holder. Despite his effort to hide it, she knew it was a one-hundred-dollar bill.

Reaching for her hand, he helped her out of her seat and continued to hold it as they walked side by side out of the restaurant. She felt so safe in the presence of this charming man who's piercing blue eyes she could never tire of. His big hand gently enveloped hers, yet she could still feel his power as he led her back to the idling town car. They'd been dining for well over an hour, and she couldn't help but wonder how much he paid his driver to sit waiting patiently for so long.

The back of the town car was filled with a mixture of laughter and mild flirtation as they zipped back to Jenna's apartment complex. Zane found Jenna's case of alcohol-induced giggles to be quite entertaining, and the occasional chuckle from Carl, his driver, indicated that he also found her amusing.

The town car pulled alongside her building, and Zane helped her out as she'd anticipated. Recognizing that she was still a bit too buzzed to attempt a flight of stairs with heels on, she kicked them off and carried them as Zane stayed one step behind her with a hand hovering behind her back. She noted his protective gesture and thanked him as they made their way up to the second floor. Standing outside her apartment door, they both searched for the right words to express their goodbyes.

"I can't thank you enough for tonight," Jenna smiled as they stood close to each other, holding hands. "It was absolutely perfect."

"I should be the one thanking you," he replied, returning the smile. "You're truly exquisite and also the first woman I've ever met who's worthy of that word."

"Oh, stop..." she blushed, playfully batting at his shoulder.

In an unexpected move, he quickly wrapped a strong arm around her waist and pulled her even closer to him. Before she could register what was happening, he leaned in and placed his soft lips to hers in a gentle kiss. She was so caught off guard that she clumsily dropped the clutch and heels she'd been holding, and they both laughed while the tips of their noses remained touching.

"Oops," she smiled as she grabbed the lapels of his suit jacket and pressed him into her for another kiss, this one far longer and much more passionate. Jenna could feel her heart pounding as their lips locked and their tongues danced together intimately.

"I haven't even left, and I want to see you again," he breathed, holding her tightly and resting his forehead on hers.

"I'd like that," she replied softly, soaking in his scent.

"When?" he asked eagerly. "Is tomorrow too soon?"

"Tomorrow's fine," she answered, affectionately placing her hand on his cheek. "Perfect, really. I have some schoolwork to finish, but I'll be free after that."

"Does 6:00 pm give you time?"

"That's fine. What did you have in mind?" she smiled warmly as she stared into his captivating eyes.

"I'd like to do dinner again, but with a different spin this time," he grinned. "I want to cook for you. No fancy restaurants. No master chefs. Just me making you dinner at my place. Then perhaps a movie, if you're up for it."

"Gorgeous, talented, successful, and you can cook?" she commented in jest. "Is there anything you can't do, mister?"

"Hey, I never said I can cook well," he laughed.

"Fair enough," she shot back. "Okay, dinner at your place it is."

"I'll pick you up at 6:00 pm," he told her, lovingly caressing her back.

"You know I can drive, right?" she joked.

"I know, I know. But it's a bit of a drive, and they aren't exactly giving gas away these days," he replied.

"Okay, deal," she conceded. Given the sorry state of her car, she knew it wasn't wise to drive it farther than absolutely necessary. She also had to admit that being chauffeured around town was something she could definitely get used to.

After a final long kiss goodbye, Jenna watched as Zane bounded down the stairs to the town car below, pausing to shoot her a smile and a small wave before climbing into the back. She picked up the clutch and heels she'd dropped, rooted to find her keys, and with her hands shaking from the excitement of the evening, she fumbled her way through, unlocking her front door. Leigh was still gone, which wasn't unusual for a Saturday night. Her friend had more of a social life than her and typically spent her weekends partying it up somewhere.

Exhausted from the evening and the wine, Jenna hurried through her nightly routine before sinking into bed. Clutching a pillow tightly and wishing it was Zane, she recounted the evening in her mind as she quickly drifted off to sleep.

Chapter Eight

The following day, she awoke with a mild hangover to find a text message from Zane thanking her once again for a wonderful time. He'd sent it a half hour after dropping her off the night before, but she'd been sound asleep by then.

She hastily replied, and he returned the text within minutes. They spent the morning casually texting each other as she straightened up the apartment and shook the rest of her headache. After a warm shower and two cups of coffee, she spent four hours finishing a school assignment due later that week.

She could have finished it sooner but found herself distracted by thoughts of Zane's gorgeous face, hypnotic eyes, and contagious laugh. Their dinner date replayed in a constant loop while she worked on adding textures to the polygonal model she'd created.

Satisfied with the finished results and with a few hours to burn until her date, she ventured into the living room, where she found Leigh curled up on the couch in front of the muted television. Jenna had woken briefly at 5:00 am when she'd heard the familiar sound of Leigh drunkenly staggering into the apartment, and by the looks of it, the girl was nursing a hangover that was much worse than hers had been.

"Shoot me," she croaked as she moved her legs so Jenna could sit beside her.

"I take it you had a fun night?" Jenna asked, staring blankly at the cartoon flashing on the television.

"Frat party. I got all sorts of fucked-up," Leigh groaned. She placed a hand over her sensitive eyes to shield her from the light. "I don't even remember how I got home."

"So, basically, it was your average Saturday night?" Jenna joked. Her friend raised her other hand to playfully flip her off.

"Fuck you, dude," Leigh smirked.

"I was hungover this morning, too," Jenna casually inserted as a coy way of steering a conversation.

"You?" Leigh removed the hand from her eyes to look at Jenna incredulously.

"Yeah, I went on a date last night and had a little too much wine. My bad," she smiled.

"Shut the fuck up!" Leigh burst as she sat up slightly. "You went on a date? No fucking way."

"Way," Jenna's grin widened.

"With who? I want details, woman," Leigh demanded, her hangover taking a back seat to her curiosity.

"Oh, no big deal, just the president of a major marketing firm," Jenna boasted, adding, "And he offered me a job."

"No fucking way," Leigh repeated. "How did you meet this guy?"

"It's a long story, but he's absolutely amazing. He took me to that Primavera restaurant downtown."

"I've heard of that place," Leigh nodded. "Very fancy. Sounds like he has money."

"He does okay for himself," Jenna shrugged.

"Is he hot?" Leigh asked excitedly.

"Oh my God, he's gorgeous," Jenna beamed as she placed her hands over her heart. "He looks like a friggin' model."

"So, let me get this straight. He's loaded, and he's hot?"

"Basically, yes," Jenna gloated.

"That's it, you're marrying him," Leigh playfully insisted.

"Shush," Jenna giggled. "We actually have a lot in common. He's extremely talented, charming, funny—"

"I thought you said you have a lot in common?" Leigh interrupted to tease.

Jenna burst out in laughter. "Somebody's got jokes."

"Well, I'm glad you got out for once," Leigh remarked sincerely. "I was beginning to worry about you."

"I know you were," Jenna replied appreciatively. "Oh, and we're going out again tonight!"

"Whoa! Two nights in a row? Damn, girl."

For the next hour, Jenna gave her friend a play-by-play of the incredible evening she'd had with Zane Talbot. At the same time, Leigh hung on to every word. Leigh attempted to share the events of her evening as well but wasn't able to recall much, thanks to the extraordinary amount of alcohol she'd downed. Jenna was thrilled she finally had time to catch up with her friend, especially now that she had some exciting news to share for once. She hadn't gotten to see her much since Leigh had switched her schedule around to accommodate her evening classes at the community college. Leigh always invited her out on weekends, but Jenna wasn't much of a partier and chose to relax at home with a good book instead.

When 4:30 p.m. rolled around, Jenna began readying herself without the painstaking effort she'd made the night before. She was ready by 5:30 pm, opting to wear a pair of jeans and a nice button-up shirt as opposed to anything fancy.

Zane had reiterated through text message that they wouldn't be going out and that she needn't worry about dolling herself up. She was perfectly fine with that and felt much more comfortable dressing down for this second date. She rejoined Leigh on the couch and spent the next half hour listening to her groan about her headache as she mindlessly flipped through the channels.

With the same punctuality of the previous night, Zane arrived a hair before 6:00 p.m., and Leigh's curiosity bested her hangover. She forced herself into a seated position, ran her fingers through her hair, and readjusted her shirt with a tug as Jenna hurried to answer the door. It was her first time seeing him without a suit, but he was still magnificently dressed in a white polo shirt that was tucked into his khaki slacks and held in place by a brown leather belt. He'd replaced his gold Rolex with a silver one, and the Italian loafers he wore looked like they oozed money. As usual, not a single hair was out of place. He greeted her with his sparkling blue eyes and perfect smile. She invited him into the modest apartment and introduced him to Leigh.

"Hi, you're really hot," Leigh blurted as he leaned in to shake her hand. Her hazel eyes were wide with awe, clearly taken with how handsome this man actually was. Zane laughed heartily at her unexpected comment.

"Leigh!" Jenna smiled in nervous embarrassment.

"Hey, I like a woman who speaks her mind," Zane smirked, unfazed by Leigh's remark.

Dragging him away from her uncouth friend, Jenna gave him a brief tour of the apartment and hesitantly showed him the small workstation she'd set up in her bedroom. Her computer was outdated, her desk cluttered, and her software largely bootleg. However, Zane looked at it affectionately while recounting how similar his setup looked when his business was in its nascent stages.

Heading back to the living room, Zane said a polite goodbye to Leigh as Jenna grabbed her purse. She guided Zane out the front door and turned to tell her friend not to wait up. With Zane just out of sight, Leigh signaled her approval of him by using her hand to fan her face while mouthing the words "holy shit." Jenna smiled, rolled her eyes, and headed out the door.

"Your roommate's quite the character," Zane chuckled as the town car rolled out of the parking lot, the two seated closely in its familiar back seat.

"That girl says whatever she's thinking, but she means well," Jenna explained apologetically.

"I should set her up with Phil Miller," Zane joked.

"Yeah…" she replied flatly, unamused by his quip.

"No?" he asked, raising his brow in curiosity.

"About that," she began apprehensively. "I'm not so sure that guy means well."

"What do you mean?"

"Eh, forget it," she waved dismissively, suddenly unsure if now was the right time to mention Phil's despicable behavior.

"No, tell me," Zane persisted as he reassuringly placed his hand on her knee.

There was a long pause as Jenna debated how to approach the subject. She didn't want to cause trouble within the firm and opted to downplay the incident in Phil Miller's office.

"Let's just say he doesn't seem to understand the concept of 'personal space,'" she finally answered with a forced chuckle.

"What do you mean by that?" Zane prodded.

"The guy just gives me the creeps, is all," she shrugged.

"I told you he's kind of a schmuck," Zane sighed. "I've had trouble with him before."

"Oh?"

"Yeah, I had to shell out quite a bit of dough to avoid a hefty sexual harassment suit, thanks to him," he divulged. "That was a few years ago, but he seems to have cleaned up his act since then."

"Let's just forget it for now," she smiled, "and enjoy our evening."

She moved her hand to his cheek to guide his mouth to hers, kissing him deeply and feeling her anger vanish.

"I could get used to that," he breathed.

"Is that so?" she giggled, their lips meeting again.

As the car sped across town for over twenty-five minutes, Jenna couldn't help but notice they'd made their way into the Catalina Foothills, one of Tucson's most affluent communities. She held Zane's hand as she watched Arizona's beautiful pastel sunset through the window while also taking note of the gorgeous homes they were cruising past.

"This is it," Zane announced as he helped her out of the car and motioned towards his home. Jenna's jaw dropped at the sight of his sprawling estate.

She'd never seen such beautiful architecture in person before and gasped while processing the sheer size of the sprawling adobe estate. Its four towering columns looked as though they were guarding the large, solid oak double doors they stood in front of. An elegant illuminated fountain in the middle of the circular driveway was situated behind them, the water spurting from its top forming a pool in the first tier and trickling its way down to the larger second tier and even larger third.

"Jesus Christ," Jenna muttered while taking in the elegance surrounding her. The entire property radiated wealth. She always wondered who lived in these lavish foothill homes at the base of Mt. Lemmon, Tucson's landmark mountain, and now she knew.

"I know, it's kind of a fixer-upper," Zane joked, breaking the silence that had fallen at the sight of his posh dwelling.

Hand in hand, he led her inside, where Jenna found the interior every bit as breathtaking as the exterior. The foyer was lined with marble pedestals, each one topped with an exquisite sculpture of unthinkable worth. A huge, original oil painting in the same vein as the famous depiction of George Washington crossing the Delaware hung from the wall just to her right, and she stood admiring its authentic brush strokes in awe.

"You'll see a lot of artwork like this throughout the house," Zane commented as he stood beside her. "My father was a Revolutionary War junkie. He actually left this piece for my brother, but when he died, it made its way to me."

"This place…" Jenna stammered, "This place is beautiful."

"You realize this is just the entrance, right?" Zane joked, prompting a playful slap to his chest from Jenna.

He guided her through the enormous home and into the spacious kitchen, giving her a brief history of the estate along the way while she listened in fascination. He'd had the house custom-built four years earlier in celebration of securing his one-hundredth client, and he'd spared no expense. In her wildest dreams, she'd never envisioned stepping foot in such a luxurious setting. She was out of her element, yet she felt right at home with Zane by her side. He spoke to her in his deep, soothing voice as he began preparing dinner.

"I hope you like chicken, but if you don't, I'll whip us up something else," he said as he searched the cabinets for his cookware, looking totally lost in the process.

"I'm getting the feeling you don't cook too often," Jenna commented, watching him bumble around clumsily.

"You could say that," he replied, cracking an egg with a focused determination on his face, his tongue peeking out as he concentrated with all his effort.

"Three more to go. I got this," he said as he caught Jenna watching him adoringly.

"This has to be one of the cutest things I've ever seen," she chuckled while placing a hand over her mouth to hide her smile. "Have you ever done this before?"

"Nope!" he exclaimed proudly. "Thank God for Google," he quipped, causing Jenna's chuckle to turn into a fit of laughter.

"You're in such amazing shape, though," she said while admiring the strong arms stretching the sleeves of his polo shirt. "What do you eat, boy?" she asked, rising an octave.

"If it weren't for protein shakes, canned and frozen food... I think I'd starve to death," he said humorously. "If my microwave ever broke, I'd probably kill myself," he added, evoking another burst of laughter from Jenna.

"You're ridiculous," she grinned. She watched him fumble with a whisk and attempt to beat the four eggs he'd successfully cracked. "You know I can help you, right?" she offered, but he held up a hand to ward off her advances.

"No, no, no," he insisted as he began draping the thinly-cut chicken breasts into a bowl of flour. "This is your night. I want you to just relax while I do all the work."

"Yes, sir," she replied with a mock salute. He divulged even more details of his personal life as he continued preparing the meal.

"Being a military guy, my dad was fairly disciplined and tried to keep himself healthy. He'd start off every morning with one hundred push-ups. I followed his lead and started doing them as well when I was around fourteen. Joined a gym when I was seventeen. He paid for the membership thinking I was strengthening up to join the Marines."

"That explains those muscles," Jenna commented, taking a seat on one of the kitchen island's bar stools. She watched his hands work their magic as the meal began to take shape.

"Yeah, well, he still passed away at only fifty-six," Zane continued. "His health really started to decline when he hit fifty, and he blamed it on that Agent Orange stuff they sprayed when he was in 'Nam."

"I see," Jenna nodded her understanding.

"Now I just work out here. I expanded the pool house out back and set up a nice home gym. You met my driver, Carl. He's actually an old family friend. He needed a job, so I also set up a small guest house for him out back. I let him stay there in exchange for his services."

"That's really nice of you," Jenna smiled.

"He's a bit irritable sometimes but a good guy. Anyhow, I'll give you the grand tour after dinner."

With the chicken breaded and ready to go, he placed it in the preheated oven and sat on the stool next to hers. He shared more about his life before probing into hers as it cooked. She told him about the gang violence and drug abuse she'd grown up around and how she'd never known her father.

She'd touched on these things the night before but expounded on them as he held her hand and listened with a look of compassion. She told him about the two robberies she'd been involved in and how exhilarating it felt to finally escape that life. She omitted her virginity, fearing it would somehow scare him away. Thankfully, he didn't ask much about her dating life.

Dinner was a resounding success, and Jenna could tell Zane was proud and relieved that he had actually accomplished it. He'd confessed that his back-up plan had been to order a pizza, but as luck would have it, his chicken parmesan was edible and delicious. He'd even prepared a small side salad, and she forgave the garlic bread for being store-bought.

As promised, a tour of the estate followed the meal. Even though Zane claimed it was the "short tour," it still took nearly an hour. The impressive library, as did the heated Grecian swimming pool, took her breath away. As much as she wanted a simple life, she had to admit that soaking up the sun poolside with a good book sounded fantastic.

The tour ended in the custom-built theater Zane had added to the home two years prior. It was dimly lit with a row of soft lights illuminating the small aisle on the right side of the room, and the twelve reclining seats lent to the authentic cinema feel.

A grand 154" projection screen was mounted to the back wall, with framed movie posters hanging on both sides of the room. In four years, Zane confessed as he let Jenna choose their seats. He hadn't invited many people into his home. He'd been so focused on expanding his business, he went on, that he'd become somewhat of a recluse. Aside from his niece, who insisted on repeated private viewings of *Frozen* on his big screen, Jenna had been the first woman to even step foot in the sanctuary that was his private cinema.

"I'll be back in five minutes; don't go anywhere," he said as he motioned for her to remain seated. He quickly bolted from the room only to return a few minutes later with a bowl of popcorn in one hand and gripping two cans of soda in the other. She couldn't contain her smile. She'd never had a man treat her so well or seem so thoroughly enthralled by her company.

"Thank you," she said as she cracked open her drink. "And how did you know I love popcorn?" she grinned.

"Lucky guess," he shrugged, sliding a small remote out of the front pocket of his pants. With the press of a button, the lights dimmed even lower, and the projector mounted to the ceiling behind them clicked on.

"Showtime!" he announced as the movie began to roll. Her grin widened when she realized he'd put on *Breakfast at Tiffany's*, one of her favorites, and she was pleasantly shocked to learn it was one of his favorites as well. He'd grown up watching it with his mother, he explained, and those memories gave the timeless classic a special place in his heart.

Together, they recited the film's most memorable lines while making short work of the popcorn. Halfway through the movie, she flipped up the armrest that had been dividing them and scooted closer to Zane, resting her head on his muscular chest as he wrapped a strong arm around her. Even over the bass from the surround sound system, she could hear his heart beating fast. When he caught her looking up at him, he returned her gaze with a warm smile.

"I swear you're too good to be true," she glowed.

Reaching for the remote he'd placed on the seat next to him, he lowered the system's volume and looked at her affectionately while tenderly brushing her cheek with the back of his hand.

"I could say the same."

Lowering his mouth to hers while dropping the remote back onto the empty seat, he lifted her chin with his strong yet gentle hand and pressed his lips against hers. The slow, deliberate kiss quickly escalated, their mouths parting and tongues mingling passionately. She straightened herself in her seat and placed her hand against his powerful chest as they kissed, and he continued to caress her warm cheek with the back of his hand as their mouths remained locked.

She instigated what happened next by lowering her hand onto his leg and rubbing it slowly. When she brushed his upper thigh, she could feel his hips thrust upwards slightly and knew he was every bit as aroused as she was. Her black lace panties were already wet but dampened more as he daringly touched her breast and lightly rubbed her through her shirt. She moaned softly as his kisses trailed down to her neck, and when she felt a bulge in her hand, she noticed she'd unknowingly cupped his crotch.

As she squeezed it, the kisses he'd been showering her neck with paused long enough for him to let out a slight groan that sounded like a mixture of pleasure and pain. She could tell he was quite well endowed, which came as no surprise given his impressive frame. His hard shaft was practically bursting through his zipper, and she imagined it had to be quite uncomfortable for him.

As she rubbed him through his pants, he managed with relative ease to undo the top three buttons of her shirt. He slid his hand inside, tugging the left cup of her bra down to expose a hard nipple. He pinched it gently between his fingers, sending a surge of pleasure shooting through her body, and she moaned even louder as he lightly licked the sensitive skin just behind her ear. Breathing heavily, her chest heaving in excitement, she tightened her grip on his crotch and heard him groan again as his erection fought to break free. Leaning forward, she fumbled with the button on his slacks but, in her nervous excitement, couldn't get it undone.

"Take it out," she heard herself whispering and felt his hand slip away from her breast.

"Are you sure?" he asked, panting in arousal and eyes full of lust.

"Yes, take it out," she breathed with a slight nod, watching as he hastily yanked the button free and unzipped his pants. Tugging his slacks down slightly, his boxer briefs along with them, she gasped as his erect cock sprang into sight.

"Jesus," she gasped in awe as she stared at its size. Courtesy of the internet, she'd seen more than her fair share of penises in her life. Yet, aside from men occasionally flashing her in her old neighborhood, she'd never seen one up close and in such an intimate setting.

Even with the low lighting, she could clearly see that his cock was more prominent than she'd anticipated, and now that it had been freed from its khaki confinement, it was finally able to grow to its fullest. She guessed it to be around eight inches but was more shocked by its thick girth. With the moment feeling right and unable to control her curiosity and her hormones, she placed her small hand around it. It had taken her twenty-four years, but she'd finally touched her first cock and was both surprised and turned on by how hard it was. She gently stroked it up and down as he threw his head back and moaned in pleasure.

She had no idea what she was doing, but by the noises he was making, she could only assume she was doing something right. He placed one hand lightly on her back while the other gripped his seat's armrest tightly. Her heart raced, and her mind flooded with thoughts as she continued to move her hand up and down the length of his cock. She'd only known this man for a short amount of time, yet she was so immensely attracted to him and trusted him so fully that she couldn't resist touching him. The entire moment felt surreal.

"Holy... f... f... fuck that feels so g... good," he stammered as she jerked him harder and faster while watching his face react to her touch.

"You like that, baby?" she asked without thinking, only to be taken aback by her own words. She'd never been an overly sexual girl, but something about this man brought out a carnal appetite she couldn't deny or control. Her soaked panties were a good indicator of the years of pent-up sexuality now pouring out of her.

"Mmhmm," he uttered before turning his head to find her lips again. Their tongues swirled together as she worked his solid shaft, twisting and squeezing as she tugged away at him. She was aware of a slight wetness on her hand but didn't think he'd gotten off yet. She'd once read about pre-cum, and could only assume this must be it.

"Take this off," he whispered, yet remained commanding as he tugged the bottom of her shirt. She hesitated slightly at the realization that no man had ever seen her topless before, yet found herself too aroused to defy him. His cock stood throbbing in anticipation as he watched her undo the remaining three buttons, then pull the shirt down around her shoulders before removing it completely.

She blindly tossed it into the row of seats before them and reached around her back to unhook her bra. He watched, his cock glistening with the identified pre-cum, as she threw it aside and sat with her full, perky breasts exposed. No man had ever seen them before, and revealing them for the first time filled her with a giddy excitement.

Leaning in, Zane suckled a sensitive, dark nipple as she held onto the back of his head and felt his tongue swirling around her areola. She never knew such a sensation existed and panted heavily while running her fingers through his thick, dark hair. He slipped a hand between her legs, and she instinctively spread them, granting him access to her most intimate area. It was another first for her as he rubbed her wet crotch through her jeans while she purred in lust, finding his cock again with her other hand and stroking it lightly.

Their pheromones mingled in a chemical waltz, Zane mouthing Jenna's breast hungrily while she jerked his thick shaft. He gently suckled her hard nipples as her breathing intensified, and when he moved to unbutton her jeans, she stopped him by pushing him back into his seat. As much as she ached to feel him inside of her, she wasn't ready to give herself to him yet. Still, she wanted to please him, and since she'd already experimented with her hands, she felt brave enough to take things one step further.

Don't even think about it, she told herself as her heart continued to pound. Just do it! Don't chicken out. You're an adult. Do it now.

She flashed him a seductive smile before kissing his soft lips again, her hand still working his impressive member as her tongue explored his mouth. Without warning, she broke the kiss and moved her head down to his lap, taking him deeply and tasting his salty pre-cum as he let out a loud groan. With one hand gliding up and down his shaft and the other gently cupping his balls, she sucked him eagerly while he vocalized his approval. He was so thick that it was all she could do to fit him in her mouth, and she gagged slightly when his length hit the back of her throat. As before, she relied on Zane's reactions to gauge how well she was doing, and his loud moans indicated that she was doing quite well indeed.

"That's it, baby. Don't stop. That feels so good," he breathed. A strong hand caressed her back while the other clenched the outer armrest. Her eyes began to water as she choked on his size, and she found herself wondering if that was normal. She typically tuned out when her friends would talk about sex, and she wasn't much for pornography.

She now regretted this, as it left her in the unenviable position of learning as she went along. She whirled her tongue around the head of his cock as she continued gently stroking him with her small hand, and the loudness of his grunts and writhing of his hips told her that he was close to climax. He knew it, too, and grabbed his cock out of her mouth.

"I don't want to cum yet," he said softly before kissing her again with unprecedented passion. "I want you," he added as his hand found her crotch and began rubbing it once more. This time, she didn't stop him and let out a lustful whimper as his fingers pressed against her clit. She masturbated regularly, typically in the shower, but that paled compared to the sensation she was feeling now.

Unable to withstand her arousal any longer, she quickly unbuttoned her pants while simultaneously kicking off her shoes. She slid her jeans down around her ankles, pulled them off with her feet, and sat wearing only her soaked black lace panties. Starting at her heaving bare breasts, Zane delicately traced the back of his fingers down her body until he reached her inner thigh. Their bodies were illuminated only by the flickering of the muted movie, yet he could see the contrast of his white skin against her ebony complexion and smiled at the sight.

Okay, this is too far now, Jenna told herself. What are you doing? Put your pants back on. Get dressed. Get out of here. Don't do this.

Yet she couldn't. The energy between them was too magnetic, and she could not protest as he suckled one of her dark, hard nipples in his mouth again. Then, pulling her panties aside, he slid his thick middle finger inside her wet hole. She gasped at the feeling, her hand clamping tightly to his shoulder as he moved in and out of her. The sensation far eclipsed that of her tried-and-true sex toy she'd ordered online three years earlier and only made her want more. He slipped his finger out to find it dripping with her warm juices and, without deliberation, placed it in his mouth to suck it clean while she watched in torrid awe.

His lips met hers again, and she could faintly taste her own flavor in his mouth as he moved his hand back down to fondle her swollen clit. Sparks shot through her body, her moans growing louder as his pace picked up, rubbing her harder and faster as she coated his hand with her cum. So aroused she could no longer contain herself, and needing to feel his thick cock inside of her, she slid off her panties and once again pushed him back into his seat to straddle him.

Stop! Stop! Stop! The angel of reason cried out in her mind, while the demon of temptation countered with, Just do it and get it over with already. You're a woman, not a child. If you're going to lose your virginity, who better to take it than this gorgeous rich guy who's treated you with nothing but respect?

She positioned herself on top of him, hovering over his cock while her inner conflict rolled on.

Enough already. You've known this guy, what, a week? Get dressed. Go home. No, don't go home. Sit on his dick right now and become a woman, for Christ's sake.

"Are you okay?" Zane panted, looking up at her with his hypnotic blue eyes that were brimming with lust and anticipation.

"Yes, I'm fine," she smiled as she leaned in to kiss his soft lips. It was too late to back out now, and her surging hormones wouldn't allow it even if she wanted to. They had an undeniable sexual chemistry, and she wasn't sure if she'd ever find a connection this strong with another man. His hands locked tightly onto her round ass as he sat staring into her brown eyes, her lengthy hair, a tussled mane falling halfway down her back.

"Wait..." Zane panted while Jenna readied herself to take him inside her waiting gash. "I don't have a condom," he blurted.

Arousal clouding her judgment, Jenna ignored his words and slowly lowered herself onto his thick shaft, wincing as her tight hole stretched to accommodate his girth.

"Fuck, you're so big," she breathed, settling onto Zane and feeling every inch of his big cock filling her. Jenna moved her hips rhythmically as his cock slid in and out of her. In front of them, Audrey Hepburn silently mouthed dialogue on the theatre's projection screen. She'd heard the first time would be painful, but that pain quickly subsided and turned to pleasure as she rode him. Within seconds, an intense orgasm rocked her body, and the room filled with her cries of pleasure mixed with his focused, coital grunts. Their bodies rocked in unison, their faces twisted in concentration and lust as they joined together in impassioned copulation. With his hands still clenching her bare ass, Zane used his strong arms to lift Jenna up and down, his shaft plunging in and out of her while her ample breasts bounced in front of his face. He took one in his mouth, sucking a hard nipple as she continued to ride him. He sat back in his seat, causing it to recline slightly, and she gripped the headrest with each hand as she leaned over him with her hips gyrating into his.

Zane controlled their motion as Jenna grinded into his lap, taking his cock deep inside of her and covering it with her warm fluids. She could feel his width pressing against her vaginal walls as he repeatedly slammed into her, and it wasn't long before she climaxed for a second time, followed by a third. Zane's lap was drenched with her cum, and she knew by his hurried breathing that he couldn't hold out much longer either. Sliding him out and feeling a hollowness inside of her, she dropped to her knees in front of his seat and took his erect shaft in her hand. It was slick with her dripping liquids, and the natural lube helped her hands glide over his throbbing cock with ease as she jerked it.

"Cum for me, baby," she pleaded seductively as she stroked him. He sat upright in his seat, his left hand gripping her shoulder tightly as he took over the reins with his right and tugged himself to climax. He loudly bellowed as the orgasm shook his body, his warm seed shooting out in thick streams and painting her naked breasts as she knelt before him.

She was taken aback by the massive load, his cum spraying like a hose until her body was covered with his mess. Her torso was coated in his release, and even her thighs didn't escape his explosion. He'd drained every ounce of himself on her, and she looked at him with a sense of accomplishment as he sank back into his seat, fighting to regain his breath. His muscular chest heaved, and beads of sweat highlighted his brow as he panted, his cock returning to its normal, yet still impressive, size. He watched her with a satisfied gaze as she remained kneeling before him, taking in the beauty of her dark skin as it gleamed with his spent load.

"You're so goddamn beautiful," he commented while panting heavily.

"I don't know about that, but I'm definitely messy," she joked, motioning to her body.

"I'll get you a towel as soon as I can walk again," he chuckled, flipping the outer armrest back down to brace his spent body on it.

"How am I completely naked, yet you still have your damn clothes on?" Jenna pointed out with a smile while playfully tugging on the bottom of his t-shirt.

"Shit, you're right. So not fair," he replied, sitting up and pulling his shirt off. She fell silent in awe as he revealed his muscular body for the first time, his wide back working in conjunction with his powerful arms to free himself of his polo. "Here," he said tenderly while handing her the shirt, "use this."

"Are you sure?" she asked with hesitation.

"Babe, you could use the U.S. Constitution right now for all I care," he quipped. Falling back into his seat, he tucked his penis back into his boxer briefs. Jenna laughed so hard she snorted, covering her mouth with her hand as she held onto his shirt.

"You're so dumb," she teased as she began wiping away his cum. As her hormones subsided and her focus returned, the realization of what she'd just done began to sink in. She'd just lost her virginity, and although the sex was amazing, she felt herself deeply conflicted by her actions. She'd broken the promise to herself she'd worked so hard to keep, but she'd never felt this way about a man before. He'd swept in out of nowhere, completely knocking her off her feet and changing all of her resolutions in the process. Complicating things even more was that he was also her new boss.

"What's wrong?" he asked, brushing her hair from her sullen face.

"Nothing, it's just... nothing..." she trailed off sheepishly, resting her head in his lap.

"No, tell me," he insisted while he caressed her back.

"It's just… that was my first time…" she mumbled.

"Wait, what?" Zane questioned, sitting up in his seat.

"That was my first time," Jenna's muffled voice repeated, her head buried in his lap out of shame and embarrassment.

"You're telling me that was your first time… with a man?" Zane chuckled in disbelief.

"Yes, stop laughing," she answered as she lightly punched his thigh.

"Oh, wow, that's… that's…" Zane's tone turned serious as he realized she wasn't joking.

"Stupid, I know," Jenna sighed, suddenly emotional and fighting back the urge to cry.

"No, no, no, it's not stupid!" Zane assured her as he bent down and kissed the back of her head softly.

"I'm not a prude or anything…" she began. "I just wanted to wait until I finished school and had a career."

"That's really respectable," Zane replied with sincerity.

"Plus, I'd never met anybody I really liked," Jenna confessed.

"So you're saying you really like me?" Zane asked with a hopeful grin.

"I thought it was obvious," Jenna shot back, her voice still slightly muffled.

"I hope you didn't have sex with me just because I gave you a job," he worried as he ran his fingers through her hair. He hoped his words wouldn't offend her. Thankfully, they didn't.

"I slept with you because I'm wildly attracted to you," she blurted.

"There's definitely something between us, isn't there?" Zane smiled while he gently rubbed her scalp.

"I'd say so," she purred beneath him with her head still on his lap.

"I can't believe I was your first," he remarked. "I feel honored. Wow."

"Well, believe it, mister."

"Are you okay? I mean, I know a girl's first time is kind of a big deal. Did I hurt you? Can I get you anything?"

"You're too sweet," she smiled as she rose to kiss him. "I'm fine, really."

"I just have to say... I would have never guessed that was your first time. You're goddamn amazing," Zane chuckled. "Holy shit."

"Really?" Jenna asked. She took a seat on his lap and wrapped her arms around his neck.

"Yes, really."

"Well, I'd been holding it in my entire life," she laughed, wiping her damp eyes and sniffling. "I guess I had a lot of sexual frustration to release."

"I'll say!" Zane agreed as he drew her close and kissed her neck. "And I'm sorry I made such a mess. I've been so busy with work I haven't gotten off in way too long."

"It's fine, silly," Jenna blushed. "It was actually kind of hot, but don't tell anybody."

"Your secret's safe with me," Zane smirked.

"Ugh, does this screw up our work relationship? I understand if you don't want me working for you now," Jenna groaned as she touched her forehead to his and combed his dark hair with her slender fingers.

"My firm doesn't have a policy on inter-office romance," he assured with a smile while lightly rubbing her back's soft, bare skin.

"Okay, good," she returned his smile.

"Come with me," he offered, taking her hand and leading her out of the room. She protested at the theatre's exit, worried their indecency would be spotted, but he assured her the adobe estate was empty. The only person on the grounds, he reminded her, was his on-call driver, who resided in the guest house recessed some two hundred yards from the residence.

"Where are we going?" Jenna asked curiously as he led her through the giant, almost intimidating home. She followed behind him, completely naked, while he walked with his pants unbuttoned, his rugged upper body making her feel protected and safe.

Heading upstairs to the master bedroom she'd briefly seen during her tour earlier in the night, he brought her into its opulent bathroom and gestured towards the large marble shower stall that was equipped with "his and hers" shower heads.

Zane kicked his slacks off and leaned into the stall to start the dual-action shower running. Jenna could feel how quickly the water heated up, a stark contrast to the worn-out water heater in her small apartment. He held open the stall's glass door for her to step inside and followed her in, standing behind her and massaging her shoulders gently as the warm water rained down on them. There was no post-coital awkwardness in their banter as they rinsed the sex off of them, and they hadn't even finished toweling dry before finding themselves on the master bedroom's four-post king-size bed.

Over the next three hours, they made love two more times, interrupted briefly when a sudden asthma attack sent Zane running downstairs to grab Jenna's inhaler from her purse. By their second round, Jenna no longer cared if Zane emptied his seed inside of her. This handsome, charming man so smote her that her better judgment had flown out the window hours earlier, and protection had taken a back seat to feel him inside of her.

During his refractory period, as they cuddled while regaining their breath and strength, they confessed their dreams and secrets to each other. Although they came from different walks of life, they found they had a tremendous amount in common. Exhausted from the new lovemaking experience, she fell asleep in the safety of his strong arms, her mind adrift with future possibilities.

Chapter Nine

It had been two months since Jenna had begun working at Zane's firm, and she'd made the transition from burger slinger to marketing artist with relative ease. She'd finished her last day at the family-owned fast food joint with mixed feelings; part of her was scared to leave the environment she'd grown so familiar with over the last four years, and another was excited to start the next chapter of her life.

Although she'd said her heartfelt goodbyes to her manager, Juan, and her coworker, Michael, *Family Burger* was still very much of a part of her life. Zane had made good on his word by assigning her to the local burger chain's account, and she'd helped spearhead a successful new direction for their marketing.

The restaurant's revenue had increased nearly twenty percent thanks to Jenna's creative campaign, and they'd used those profits to renovate their existing locations completely. Their business was booming, and plans to launch an eleventh location on the city's east side were already in development.

However, the jump from Family Burger to Enterprise Marketing hadn't been completely seamless. Jenna and Zane had made every attempt to keep their relationship low-key, but it hadn't taken long for rumors to begin circulating. While most staff had accepted her with open arms, Jenna suspected several employees resented her rapid ascension within the firm.

In only two months, she'd already helmed her own thriving campaign, and its undeniable success had led to Zane appointing her as the new artistic head of the BMW account — the firm's largest client. While nobody showed any outright signs of hostility, she heard rumblings of favoritism but ignored them as best she could while remaining focused on her work.

Phil Miller, who had snagged BMW as a client years earlier and remained their account manager, was ecstatic to have Jenna working alongside him. Jenna, however, wasn't as thrilled. She'd kept the extent of his inappropriate advances to herself, choosing not to tell Zane about his right-hand man's persistent passes. Consequentially, she wound up paired with the chauvinistic pig. If Phil knew about her affair with their boss, he certainly did a good job turning a blind eye to it. She'd made avoiding the man a part of her daily routine, but given the nature of their working relationship, it was often impossible.

The BMW team comprised five members: one writer, two artists, Jenna as creative director, and Phil handling client relations. Jenna made every attempt to ensure that at least one other team member was accompanying her and Phil at all times. However, when that wasn't an option, she was forced to suffer through his suggestive looks and uncouth remarks that were becoming more aggressive with each passing week.

She regularly debated telling Zane about the unwanted flirtation or confronting the man herself but knew how vital Phil Miller was to *Enterprise Marketing's* continued success. Given how new she was to the firm, she thought it best to keep quiet in fear of causing tumult within the company that may somehow fall back on her. She would bide her time and speak her mind when the moment was right.

Aside from Phil, she was greatly enjoying her time with the firm. Zane kept his influence on her work to a minimum, and she appreciated him giving her the creative space she needed. While she admired and respected his abilities, she didn't need anyone holding or guiding her artistic hand. He allowed her to do her thing, and she'd proven she could hold her own within the company. As a bonus for her superb handling of the *Family Burger* campaign and as an early graduation present, Zane had surprised her with a car she'd only accepted after great protest. He'd reiterated that it was nothing fancy, but the keys to the used 2006 Lexus said otherwise. Because of her new wheels, she'd promptly scrapped her old, run-down Ford and was thankful to finally have a reliable source of transportation.

At Zane's insistence, Jenna spent most of her time at his foothill estate, where the two would fawn over each other in between making love. Jenna had developed a ferocious sexual appetite, and Zane was quite accommodating of it. They had grown inseparable, and although they hadn't spoken the words yet, it was quite obvious that they were in love.

Jenna desperately wanted to put those three words out there, but her uncertainty about how Zane would react kept them restrained. She suspected her feelings were reciprocated but didn't want to look foolish if she were wrong. Her position within the firm may have filled her with confidence, but she still couldn't shake her habit of overthinking things.

With only one month left, her time at the University was drawing to an end, yet she'd managed to keep her grades up despite her hectic schedule. Soon, she would have the degree she'd worked so hard for to go along with her charming, affluent boyfriend and promising new career. Zane had asked her to stay with the firm full-time after graduating, and Jenna gladly accepted the offer.

She fit in well with his company, even with Phil Miller's looming presence, and couldn't imagine working anywhere else. She'd achieved so much in the two short months she'd worked at *Enterprise Marketing* that starting all over again somewhere new seemed counterproductive.

Zane had also asked her to move in with him when her schooling finished, joking that it would be silly not to, considering the amount of time they spent together. After a degree of deliberation and a lengthy discussion with an understanding and supportive Leigh, Jenna began boxing up her things for the move across town.

The following month, an emotional, teary-eyed Jenna was handed her hard-earned degree as Zane, beaming with pride, looked on. She thought back to her life in Brooklyn, the rough neighborhood she'd come from, and how she'd managed to escape it, unlike so many of her family and friends. Four years earlier, she was praying for her life while being robbed in a seedy bodega. Now, thanks to her own determination and talent, she was a university graduate working for a lucrative marketing agency. She'd tried calling her mother to share her success, but unsurprisingly, there was no answer. In recent months, her mother had become increasingly harder to reach, and she'd completely lost touch with her brother.

Later that same day, a small moving truck, paid for by Zane, arrived at her apartment complex, and two men in blue coveralls loaded her boxes into the back. Four years ago, she'd driven across the country with all of her belongings squeezed into her small car, and since then, she hadn't acquired much else in terms of personal possessions. She'd purchased a full-size mattress shortly after moving in with Leigh but agreed with Zane that she'd no longer need it.

She left it behind, hoping Leigh's future roommate could use it, and held Zane's hand as she observed the men load her computer desk and remaining boxes into the truck.

With a handsome man by her side, an exciting new career, a car she didn't have to pray would start, and a bachelor's degree hanging on the wall of her new home, Jenna felt like she was living a dream. That dream, however, would soon turn into a long, dark nightmare.

Chapter Ten

"We meet again, beautiful," Phil's voice sounded as he sidled up next to Jenna by the break room's vending machine.

"Phil," she greeted flatly, refusing to make eye contact while hurrying to slide her quarters into the machine. She'd hoped to slip in and out of the break room undetected, but Phil's watchful eyes had apparently spotted her.

"You finally have me all alone," he smirked while leaning against the machine, hands casually in his pockets and eyes fixated on Jenna.

"Yay," she replied sarcastically, unamused by his attempted joke.

"Listen, why don't you come over to my place tonight so we can discuss the BMW account over dinner?" he brazenly asked with unwavering confidence.

"Are you being serious right now?" Jenna blurted as the machine dispensed the Doritos she'd been having an unusual craving for.

"Of course I am. It's been three months, and you still haven't called me," he playfully grinned as he moved closer to her. She recoiled at his approach and turned to meet his gaze with fire in her eyes.

"You do realize I live with your boss now?" she scoffed. She'd put up with his advances long enough and had finally reached her breaking point. Phil, however, remained unfazed by her bitter tone.

"Yeah, I heard about that," he chuckled. "Zane's a good guy, but come on," he added while rolling his eyes.

"What's that supposed to mean?" a flustered Jenna asked with her brow raised in irritated curiosity.

"You and him," Phil spoke softly as he inched even closer to her, "don't belong together. Face it. You're two different people. He might be into you now, but it'll never last."

Jenna could smell the faint odor of alcohol on his breath. He moved to touch her hair, and she swatted his hand away angrily. She was so upset she was shaking and could feel herself losing control of her temper.

"You don't know what you're talking about," she growled, trying to maintain her composure. She attempted to walk past him, but he quickly stepped to the side and blocked her path.

"I can give you so much more than he ever could," he announced, his tone hushed as not to be overheard.

Jenna silently prayed for somebody, anybody, to burst through the door and interrupt their uncomfortable exchange.

"Look, Phil, I'm sure you're a nice guy and all," Jenna lied in hopes of diffusing the situation, "but I'm just not into you in that way. I'm sorry."

"You shallow bitch!" he unexpectedly barked, his demeanor becoming threatening as he pointed a stubby finger in her face. She flinched at his sudden outburst, and the bag of chips she was holding fell to the ground. "You only like him because of his looks, you fucking whore," he continued in a low hiss.

"You need to back the fuck up right now," she countered as she snapped her fingers in his face, her urban patois bursting to the surface. She was taller than Phil and glared down at him as she stepped toward him to unleash her anger. "Zane's twice the man you'll ever be, and when he finds out what a sleazebag you are, you'll be lucky to have a goddamn job."

"Oh, feisty, I like that!" Phil chuckled, grinning wide as he backed up with his hands raised in mock surrender. "And you really think he'd take the word of a slut like you over a guy like me? I've done more for this company than you ever will. See, you might think you can sleep your way to the top, but it's never going to happen. Not on my watch."

"You've got some serious mental problems," Jenna spat, suddenly aware of a growing queasiness in her stomach. She'd been feeling nauseous all week, vomiting twice, and had chalked it up to food poisoning of some sort.

"Why don't you just go back to the ghetto you crawled out of?" Phil sneered, his face twisted in disgust.

"I… I… I'm going… to be sick," Jenna stammered, knees buckling as she clutched her abdomen with one hand and braced herself on a table with the other. She could feel her insides churning and knew she was going to throw up. Pushing herself past Phil, who stood with a look of confusion, she bolted from the room. She raced down the hallway and barely reached the ladies' room, where she dropped to her knees and vomited violently into the toilet.

"W-w-what the fuck?" she asked herself as her nose dripped and her eyes watered. She wiped her nose with the back of her hand, flushed the toilet, and was rising to her feet when another wave of nausea hit her. She fell to her knees again and threw up for a second time, panic setting in as she clung to the bowl and heaved. Making her way to the sink, she splashed cool water on her face and composed herself in the restroom's mirror. She knew Zane was working diligently in his office just down the hall, but she didn't want to interrupt him or cause undo concern over what she hoped was a simple stomach bug.

Acting as nonchalantly as possible, she retrieved her purse from the art room before ducking out of the building and hurrying to her car. She drove the short distance to Tucson Medical Center and checked into the emergency room with her stomach still in knots.

She kept an eye on her phone while she waited for her name to be called, hoping Zane wouldn't call or text to question her whereabouts. Thirty minutes later, a heavyset nurse guided her into a small examination room.

"Take a seat," the nurse instructed while pointing at the exam table. Jenna did as told, the table's paper lining crinkling beneath her as she hopped into position. The sizable nurse, who seemed devoid of any personality, took her blood pressure and jotted the numbers down on her clipboard. "A doctor will be with you shortly," she mumbled as she darted off.

Jenna waited anxiously to be seen, occasionally checking her phone to see if her absence had been noticed. Ten minutes later, a doctor hurried in, carrying the same clipboard the nurse had presumably handed him, and immediately began his routine line of questioning while eyeing her paperwork.

"Says here you've had an upset stomach lately?" he asked as he scrolled through her information. He was an older man. Jenna guessed him to be in his mid-fifties, and his hair had gone completely white. He looked tired, the dark bags under his eyes indicating he was at the tail end of a very long shift.

"Yes, that's right," she answered nervously. "I've been cramping pretty bad all week. I've thrown up a couple of times. I'm not sure if it's food poisoning or what."

"Well, that's what we're going to find out," he replied, glancing at her and forcing a smile. "You said this just started this week?"

"Yeah. Well, it's more like the end of last week. Came out of nowhere," she told him as he began his examination.

"I see," he muttered while looking her over. "Have you ever experienced anything like this before?"

"No, never," she shook her head.

"You've been feeling nauseous?"

"Yes," she nodded.

"Did this begin after you ate something specific?"

"I don't think so, no."

"Any other symptoms?"

"I've been pretty tired lately."

"Active sex life?"

"I... uh... yes," Jenna responded, the question clearly catching her off guard.

"There's a bathroom across the hall," the doctor sighed as he pulled a small plastic cup from the room's medical cabinet and handed it to her. "I need you to go pee in this. When you're done, hand it to a nurse and wait for me back here."

The doctor vanished as quickly as he'd appeared, leaving a concerned Jenna sitting alone with the empty cup. She crossed to the bathroom as instructed, her nerves allowing her to fill the cup easily as her overactive mind pulsed with thoughts.

Why did he ask about my sex life? Do I have an STD? Oh, God, what if I have something? Am I sick? I'm probably dying. Cancer? Don't let it be cancer. And why did he ask about my sex life? That was random.

Finished with her business, she handed the full cup to the same nurse who'd guided her to the examination room and returned to her seat on the table. Her mind continued to race as she sat waiting for what felt like hours until the doctor finally returned with the familiar clipboard under his arm.

"Well, you're not dying," he joked dryly as if he could read her mind.

"Okay..." Jenna replied, her heart pounding so loudly she thought it might burst his eardrums if he put the stethoscope to her chest.

"You're pregnant," he told her emotionlessly, scribbling a series of notes on the clipboard. Jenna sat in stunned disbelief for a long moment while processing his words.

"That's… that's impossible," she gulped. "That can't be right."

"Well, it is. A simple urine test confirmed it. Honestly, I could tell the second I saw you," he said as he continued to write.

"You could?" she questioned, still unable to wrap her mind around the diagnosis.

"I've been at this a while," he smiled warmly while looking at her with a fatherly comfort. It was the first genuine emotion he'd shown, and the unexpected act of kindness immediately helped to calm her. Clearly, the good doctor sensed her panic, and although he was obviously exhausted, he'd mustered the strength to lend her the emotional support she desperately needed. "I've seen it a million times."

"How is this possible?" she asked out of denial.

"Well, either you're the next Mother Mary," he chuckled, "or I'd say you've been having some sex."

"But I've been using protection," she explained as her eyes began to well with tears. After giving herself to Zane and realizing how foolish they'd been to skip any form of prevention, she'd visited Planned Parenthood and began taking birth control. Even knowing the pills would take effect within a week, she still insisted that Zane wear a condom for the first month just to be on the safe side.

"Nothing's one hundred percent," the doctor shrugged and handed her a tissue.

"How far along am I?" she sniffed while dabbing her eyes.

"We'd need a blood or ultrasound test for that," he answered apologetically. "If you don't have a local physician, I'd suggest you find one. We can refer you to an obstetrician."

"Thank you," she wheezed as he helped her down from the table. Reaching into her purse, she found her inhaler and let its albuterol work its magic.

"It'll be a bit of a wait, but we can get you the ultrasound today, and you'll know the baby's exact age," he offered.

"I can't today, but I'll schedule an appointment with somebody soon," she replied, knowing she'd already been missing from work long enough.

After receiving a list of recommended obstetricians, she made her way back to the car Zane had graciously surprised her with and sat in a silent, motionless daze while tears slowly streamed down her cheeks. She replayed the news in her mind, unable to believe the cruel hand fate had dealt her. Given the birth control she'd been taking and the condoms she'd made him wear until she felt confident the pills were doing their job, it was clear that this pregnancy was the direct result of her first and only night of unprotected intimacy with Zane. She'd fought hard to avoid this exact situation by abstaining from sex, and by giving in to temptation, she'd managed to lose her virginity and wind up pregnant at the same time. It didn't seem fair, and onlookers would have deemed her crazy when she unexpectedly began to pound on the steering wheel while sobbing uncontrollably and unleashing a barrage of profanity.

Five minutes passed before Jenna managed to calm herself. The time on her car's stereo display read 3:06 p.m. She knew her former roommate's routine well and knew her friend would likely be home. Leigh's shift at *Family Burger* ended at 2:00 p.m., and the girl typically killed time at the apartment before heading to her 6:00 p.m. evening class at the community college. Needing the support of her only true female friend, she made the short commute to the familiar complex she'd lived in for nearly four years and was relieved to see

Leigh's car in her designated parking spot. She didn't bother calling or even texting to announce her arrival. Instead, she bolted up the flight of stairs and pounded frantically on the door.

"Way to scare the shit out of me," Leigh jokingly answered, her face and tone abruptly turning serious at seeing her friend's distress. "Hey, what's wrong?" she asked as Jenna stormed past her into the apartment and sunk down on the broken-in sofa that had also become a good friend over the years.

Jenna said nothing for a long moment, sitting silently and staring vacantly at the carpet before suddenly bursting into tears. Leigh rushed to her side and wrapped a comforting arm around her distraught friend's shoulders.

"What is it?" a concerned Leigh questioned while she began to rub Jenna's back in an attempt to comfort her.

"I'm… I'm…" Jenna began but found herself unable to speak the words.

"Shhh… It's okay," Leigh assured her soothingly. "Just tell me what's going on. What happened?"

"I'm pregnant!" Jenna blurted with a wail, burying her face in her hands and weeping loudly.

"Jesus," Leigh quietly gasped. "With Zane's baby?"

"Yes, with Zane's baby!" Jenna cried as she lifted her head to shoot Leigh an irritated look. "Who else?"

Her eyes were red and puffy, her cheeks flushed, and her nose ran slightly. She looked like a complete mess as rivulets of tears ran down her face.

"Damn, that's… wow," Leigh muttered, unsure how to console her friend. "I take it you just found out?"

"Mmmhmm," Jenna sniffled. Leigh hurried to fetch her a box of tissues and quickly returned to her side.

"How far along are you?" Leigh asked while Jenna wiped her nose and dabbed the tears from her cheeks.

"Three months, I think," Jenna's trembling voice answered. "God, I'm so stupid. We didn't use protection the first night we had sex. I mean, we have every other time, but not that first night."

"That's really shitty," Leigh remarked, still uncertain how to reply and treading as lightly as possible.

"I'm that girl who gets pregnant her first time," Jenna sighed. "What are the odds of that?"

Thinking Jenna had misspoken or that she'd simply misheard her, Leigh didn't probe and steered the conversation in a different direction.

"Does Zane know?"

"No. I just found out," Jenna sniffled again. "I don't know if I can tell him. He's such a great guy, but he's never said anything about wanting kids, and this could seriously mess up his life. Mine, too."

"What are you going to do?" Leigh asked as she brushed Jenna's hair from her troubled face.

"I don't know." After a deliberative pause, she continued, "He can't find out. He just can't. He's trying to expand his business to the East Coast, and this will completely ruin his plans. He'll hate me."

"I'm sure he won't hate you. You're overreacting," Leigh assured her.

"Well, he'll resent me, and that's close enough," Jenna replied. "He wants to open a branch in New York soon. He's worked years for this. He won't be able to do it if he's stuck here taking care of a girl he's only been with for three months."

"What about you?" Leigh prodded as she resumed rubbing her friend's back. "What do you want to do?"

"I have no idea. I love Zane so much, but I don't think I'm ready for a baby. Not yet. Not now. Hell, I just graduated. I have a good job. One that I really like," Jenna's thoughts came pouring out. "I always imagined having a baby when I was thirty or something. This is way too soon."

"It's always way too soon," Leigh joked, hoping levity would lighten the mood. "Nobody's ever really ready. That's just how life works."

"I suppose…" Jenna nodded. She grabbed another tissue and wiped more tears from her eyes. "But I've worked so hard to get where I am, and Zane has, too. The timing is just terrible."

"Well, if you're really three months along," Leigh began hesitantly, "it's not too late to consider… other options."

"You mean an abortion?" Jenna swallowed hard as she mulled over the suggestion.

"Yeah," Leigh replied. "You'd be in and out. Zane would never have to know."

"I don't know if I could do it," Jenna shook her head with a sigh. "I'd feel so guilty. And I've never lied to Zane."

"You need to make the decision soon," Leigh pointed out. "But whatever you decide to do… I'm here for you."

She wrapped her arm around her trembling friend and held her close, the two sitting in silence as Jenna's sobbing chest heaved. The moment was interrupted by Jenna's phone alerting her to a new text message from Zane, wondering where she'd disappeared.

She replied that she'd dipped out for a late lunch and would be returning shortly. It was the first lie she'd ever told him, and it certainly didn't feel good. If she had this much trouble lying through a short text message, she didn't know if she had it in her to conceal an entire pregnancy.

Chapter Eleven

"I really need to talk to you," Ali whispered as she sidled up next to her boss with a manila folder under her arm.

After wrapping up a lengthy phone call with a potential client, Zane had ventured from his office to the firm's design studio under the guise of overseeing the progress of his staff's various projects. His real intent, however, was to steal a kiss from Jenna discreetly, yet he found her missing from her workstation.

He quickly checked the break room but didn't find her there either, and headed back into the studio, where he lingered by her computer, assuming she was using the restroom. When she still hadn't returned after ten minutes, he texted her out of worry, and she'd replied seconds later to tell him that she was grabbing a bite to eat. Relieved, he popped his cell phone back into the breast pocket of his jacket and turned his attention to the head of his accounting department.

"Do you have a second?" she asked with a look of concern.

"I do. Follow me," he politely smiled as they made their way down the hall and into his office. He closed the door behind them and gestured for her to take a seat while he took his place behind the desk.

"What seems to be the problem?" he asked, folding his hands across his lap.

"Remember those two accounts I told you about? The Kroger and Tanque Verde Ranch accounts? The missing money?"

"I do," Zane nodded.

"Well..." Ali began as she opened up the manila folder she'd been carrying. "I found one more."

She pushed her horned-rimmed glasses up with her index finger and handed three printouts to Zane. She looked at him nervously while he reviewed the information she'd presented him with.

"Interesting," he replied stoically while his blue eyes scanned the first page.

"Right? Another mystery account. This one's more recent, too. Hotel Congress. Says we spent twenty grand on their account three months ago, but there's no record of where that money went," Ali explained as she fidgeted in her chair.

"I see that," Zane muttered. He leaned back in his seat and continued to digest the documents while rubbing his chin in thought. "Hotel Congress. I didn't even know they were a client of ours."

"Me neither," Ali shrugged, "but it says Mr. Miller brought them on board."

"Indeed it does," Zane agreed as he flipped the page and spotted Phil's signature on the client contract form.

"Between this and those other two accounts, that's one hundred thousand dollars we're missing," Ali gulped.

"Wait, that other eighty thousand was never accounted for?" Zane asked in shocked agitation.

"That's what I'm trying to tell you," a flustered Ali squeaked.

"I assigned Phil to that months ago now," Zane hissed angrily. "He assured me he'd take care of it. He didn't stop by accounting to discuss it with you?"

"N-n-no..." Ali stuttered, her body beginning to shake with fear.

Remembering his accountant's timid, fragile nature, Zane reeled in his emotions. He straightened his tie and flashed her a fake smile as he feigned a calm composure.

"I see," he replied. "He was supposed to handle it. Perhaps it slipped his mind. I'll meet with him and get back to you."

"Thank you."

"In the meantime, don't mention a word of this to anybody, got it?" Zane insisted.

"Yes, sir," Ali nodded.

"Not one word. Not even to Phil. You keep this strictly between us," he reiterated. His eyes widened to express the importance of their confidentiality.

"Yes, sir," she repeated as she readjusted her glasses again.

Rising from his seat, he guided her out of the room and asked his secretary to summon Phil Miller. He closed his office door and returned to his desk, turning his chair to take in the beauty of the shadows falling across the city's mountainous backdrop. His view of the landscape's setting sun was short-lived, interrupted within seconds by the ringing of his office phone.

"Yes?" he answered tersely.

"Mr. Talbot, it appears Mr. Miller has left to meet with a client," his secretary's voice informed him. "I've left a message for him to contact you at his earliest convenience."

"Thank you, Sheryl," he sighed. "Just tell him to meet with me tomorrow."

Hanging up the phone, he picked up the three printouts Ali had left for him and studied them closely. His cell phone vibrated in his breast pocket, signaling that he'd received a text message. He glanced at its screen and smiled.

"Back. You miss me?" the message from Jenna read.

"You know it," he typed back. "Now get in here and show me some love."

Moments later, his door cracked open, and Jenna poked her head in to find him waiting patiently with his chair tilted back and his feet resting on his desk.

"I see you're hard at work," she joked as she entered his office and closed the door behind her. He righted his chair and placed his feet back on the floor as she crossed the room to him and took a seat on his lap.

"You're a sight for sore eyes, babe," he greeted, wrapping his strong arms around her waist and kissing her soft, full lips.

"You look stressed," she said while running her fingers through his dark hair.

"You do, too," he commented, his observant eyes locking onto hers. His intuition was too good. She'd tried to mask it, but he could clearly see her upset. "What's wrong?"

"Just some family stuff. It's nothing, really," she assured him before kissing his forehead softly.

"You want to talk about it?" he asked as he gently brushed her cheek with the back of his hand.

"I'm fine, really. I'm more worried about you," she remarked to redirect the conversation. "You never look this stressed. You're always Mr. Cool. What's the matter?"

"Just some accounting discrepancies. I'm handling it," he sighed, nuzzling her neck with his nose.

She'd proven successful in avoiding his questions for the time being. She desperately wanted to tell him about their baby but needed more time to determine the best course of action. Telling him would surely jeopardize the expansion of the company he'd worked so hard to build while simultaneously derailing her new career. Conversely, withholding the truth meant she'd have to lie to the man she'd fallen so hard for. The same man who'd been nothing but good to her. The same man she now worked for and lived with. Given how stressed he looked, she didn't want to cause him any additional burden. She was in a tough spot, and judging by his distressed eyes, so was he. No, whatever decision she reached definitely wouldn't be made in haste.

"Let me know if there's anything I can help with," she offered as he began caressing her inner thigh. She knew him well enough to know what this meant, but the news she'd been given less than two hours earlier had killed her otherwise insatiable sex drive.

Two days prior, after compulsively checking three times to ensure that his office door was locked, she'd allowed Zane to bend her over his office desk and take her from behind, trying her hardest to remain quiet as he thrust his sizable cock in and out of her. It wasn't the first time they'd had sex in his office, and she hoped it wouldn't be the last. She loved the rush of fucking in the workplace, something she never expected she'd enjoy so immensely, but the day's events had completely wrecked her mood.

"There might be something you can help with," he seductively groaned, placing her hand on his crotch. She leaned in and kissed him passionately, feeling his tongue against hers, and tightened her grip on his growing bulge.

Jenna had always welcomed his sexual advances and didn't want to arouse suspicion by denying them now. For the first time, she had no desire to feel him inside of her, yet she didn't want to leave him hanging when he clearly needed release the most. Slowly dropping to her knees, she unbuckled his belt while looking up at him with a sly grin.

After undoing the top button of his pants and tugging down his zipper, she reached into his boxer briefs and took his thick shaft in her hand. She began stroking him gently, and he closed his eyes while letting out a long, quiet moan that indicated his satisfaction.

"That's it, baby," he breathed as she licked the tip of his hard cock. "Suck it," he instructed, but he was already in her mouth before he'd finished uttering the words.

The thrill of knowing his office door was unlocked made the moment that much more exciting for them both. Zane prided himself on his professionalism but knew his secretary would never dare enter his private domain unannounced. Phil Miller was the only employee brazen enough to pull such a move, but he wasn't even in the building. Still, the possibility of somebody walking in was very real, which made the act even hotter.

Jenna took him deep in her mouth, working his shaft with her hand while Zane fought to keep his carnal grunts and groans to a minimum. They'd always been extremely vocal in their lovemaking, and keeping quiet was not something they were particularly good at. He brushed the hair from her face to watch as she sucked him, then gripped his chair's armrests tightly as she continued to please him.

"Don't stop, don't stop," he panted as her head bobbed up and down. Jenna had been quite a self-conscious lover for the first month of their relationship, worried her inexperience would somehow impede their romance. She was incredibly nervous regarding her oral abilities, but Zane had reassured her that she was quite good, and his body language seemed to support that.

"You like that, baby?" she paused to whisper, jerking his solid erection while looking up at him with her big, brown eyes. "I want you to cum for me."

"Holy shit!" he grunted as quietly as he could, his left hand moving from the armrest to clutch her right shoulder. His eyes were closed, and his face was twisted in sexual concentration. He was on the verge of an explosion, and Jenna knew it.

"That's it, give it to me," she demanded before taking him deep in her mouth again, her hand gliding along his thick member as she sucked him hard and fast. His body tensed, and he groaned low profanity as he flooded her mouth with an unexpectedly big load. It was all she could do to swallow it down, and she fought back the sudden urge to vomit. She'd never had such a visceral reaction to his cum before and realized the pregnancy was to blame for its sudden acrid taste. She glanced at the small trashcan, hugging the side of his desk as she tried to mask her sickness.

"Holy shit," she gasped as she wiped her mouth with her sleeve and managed to fake a smile, "that was a lot."

"I'd apologize if I were sorry, but I'm not," Zane joked, breathing heavily as his drained body sunk back into his seat. "That was incredible."

He stuffed his satisfied cock back into his pants, and she rested her head on his thigh while he ran his fingers through her thick hair.

"I'm sorry you're so stressed, babe," she sighed. He gently massaged her scalp the way he knew she liked it. "I hate seeing you like this."

"Right now, I'm not stressed at all," he chuckled.

"Good," she smiled up at him.

"Let me take you to dinner tonight," he insisted. "You can tell me what's going on with your family."

"Can we do it some other time?" Jenna asked, her stomach still churning and mentally exhausted from the emotional day she'd been having. "My tummy's kind of been a mess today, and I still have a ton of work to finish up."

"Aw, sweetie, if you're not feeling well, just go home and get some rest," Zane replied as his hand moved from her head to her back and began rubbing it lightly.

"Can't, too much to do," she groaned while she rose to her feet and readjusted her shirt. "This BMW account's no joke."

"If it's too much, I can move you to something else," Zane offered. Following her lead, he zipped his pants back up and buckled his belt.

"No, no, I can handle it," Jenna assured him. "The team's come up with some great new concepts for their campaign. We just need to finish up the artwork so we can present it to them next week."

"Just let Phil do the talking, and I'm sure they'll buy whatever you show 'em," Zane remarked. "That guy can talk his way into anything."

"Except my pants…" Jenna mumbled as she rolled her eyes.

"Wait, what?" Zane questioned, leaning forward in his chair and studying her face with his hypnotic blue eyes.

"Eh, never mind," Jenna shook her head dismissively.

"Just tell me," he persisted with a look of agitation.

"It's just… the guy's a total creep, okay? I told you that before. I know you like him, or he's good for business or whatever, but the guy's totally sketchy, and I'm convinced he's mentally unstable," Jenna finally confessed.

"I never said I liked him personally, but he's definitely done a lot for this company," Zane explained as concern spread across his face. "Did something happen?"

"It's *been* happening, Zane," Jenna blurted. "The idiot hits on me non-stop. It's every goddamn day, and I don't know if I can take it anymore. Earlier, he cornered me in the break room and said things I won't even begin to repeat. Oh, and I'm pretty sure he was drunk," she revealed.

"Ugh," Zane groaned as he shook his head in disappointment. "I'm so sorry, babe. I had no idea this was going on. I had problems with him a while back but thought he'd changed."

"Well, clearly he hasn't," Jenna fired back in a huff. "He treats me like I'm some piece of meat. I can always feel his eyes on me, making my skin crawl."

"I'll take care of it," Zane sighed. "And I apologize. I should have known better than to team you up with him."

"It's not your fault," Jenna replied. "He seems to be on his best behavior around you. But it's a whole other story when he's alone with me."

"I don't know what I'm going to do," an exasperated Zane shrugged. "He's brought in a lot of business, but I can't have him pulling this crap here. Not with you. Not with anybody. I told him before I wouldn't put up with it again."

"Again? " Jenna asked. "So this is a repeat pattern?"

"A few years ago, there was an incident with his secretary," Zane clarified. "It was the first time, and I told him it better damn well be his last."

"I see."

"How long has this been going on?" Zane demanded to know.

"Since I started working here," Jenna answered, and after a brief pause, added, "Before, actually."

"Before?" Zane burst in puzzlement.

"He's been making inappropriate comments since the first day he met me," a visibly upset Jenna snapped. "Let's just say that tour of the firm didn't end so well."

"Jesus, babe," Zane began, shooting from his chair and rushing to console her. He placed his strong hands on her shoulders and looked at her apologetically. "I wish you'd told me sooner."

"I know he's your little golden boy, so I didn't want to cause trouble," Jenna muttered as she looked away in embarrassment.

"I'll fix this, I promise," he assured her with his deep, commanding voice.

"How?" Jenna questioned with a faint hint of skepticism as she returned his gaze.

"I'm supposed to meet with him over an accounting issue tomorrow. I'll handle it when I see him. Until then, I don't want you two around each other. You're taking the day off. Relax at home while I take care of Phil," Zane instructed.

"I can't just take the day off," Jenna started to protest, "I have work to finish and—"

"That wasn't a suggestion," Zane interrupted sternly. "You're taking tomorrow off while I sort this out. You've been working hard and deserve a break anyhow."

"Okay..." Jenna quickly conceded, remembering the pressing personal matters requiring her immediate attention. Their child was growing inside of her, and she still needed to figure out what she would do about it. A day to herself, she realized, might just help her reach the decision she inevitably needed to make.

"In fact," Zane continued as he glanced at his watch, "I want you to head home right now. I won't be far behind you. I have a few phone calls to finish up here, then I'll be on my way."

"You sure?" Jenna asked. She was feeling ill again, and the chance to relax at the adobe estate she'd grown accustomed to was hard to resist.

"Yes. Phil's meeting with a client right now, and I do not know when he'll be back. I'd rather you two not be in the same building together until I've spoken with him. If he gets here before I leave, then I'll have it out with him today. If not, I'll deal with him tomorrow."

"Okay, sweetie," Jenna replied, standing on her toes to kiss his stubbly cheek. She could still taste him in her mouth and didn't think he'd appreciate a kiss on the lips.

"I'll see you in a bit, gorgeous girl," he smiled as he pulled her close and kissed her forehead.

He saw her out of his office and returned to his high-back leather chair. Turning to face the room's large plate window, he watched as shadows crept over the city's impressive mountain range again. As the sun sank lower, he silently deliberated on Phil Miller's fate.

Chapter Twelve

"Pow, pow! Gimme one more!"

Phil Miller slammed his empty glass down on the bar's countertop with such force that several patrons turned to glare at him in annoyance, all of them shocked that the glass hadn't shattered.

"Easy, pal," the burly, tattooed barkeep hissed angrily.

"Sorry, my bad," Phil replied while trying not to slur his speech.

He'd told his secretary he was leaving to meet with a client, but he desperately needed another drink after Jenna's rejection. His boss may have instated a policy three years earlier that barred alcohol from the building, but the hot shot never made it clear whether or not that ruling extended to the parking lot.

Capitalizing on this, Phil typically kept a generous amount of white rum, cleverly poured into twelve-ounce water bottles to conceal its identity, in the trunk of his silver Mercedes. Throughout the day, he'd sneak out for a few swigs, yet to the casual observer, he was merely grabbing a quick drink of water.

He'd hit his secret stash particularly hard that morning, downing an entire bottle before the clock had even struck noon. Over the last several months, his life had decayed rapidly. His girlfriend had left him for a handsome, successful lawyer, triggering a depression that saw him pack on twenty pounds. He'd developed an addiction to escorts, using them to fill the void left in both his heart and bed. He found that alcohol helped the confidence his girlfriend had crushed when she unexpectedly tossed him aside in favor of a man who looked like he'd been ripped off the cover of a romance novel.

He felt extremely under-appreciated at work, sensing his coworkers all mocked him behind his back. Since his time with Enterprise Marketing, he'd brought the firm many new clients, but nobody seemed to notice, let alone care. They all adored Zane Talbot, the supposed marketing whiz who could do no wrong, even though the man hadn't brought in any new business in months.

Phil had been doing all the work while his playboy boss had been busy romancing inner-city trash. Everyone revered Zane, and Phil suspected his chiseled good looks and undeniable charm played a large part in that. Behind his model features lay a man who wasn't nearly as talented as his sycophant lackeys made him out to be, and Phil resented him for this. However, he never let that resentment show and had become quite good at hiding his disdain for the man who'd taken him under his wing.

"One more rum and Coke, but keep it down, got it?" the bartender scowled as he placed another drink before Phil.

"You got it, chief," Phil agreed with a nod. He sucked down half of the drink while casually leaning against the bar and surveying the room. It was a seedy dive bar he'd never been to, and he stood out in his imitation Armani suit.

The bar at *Primavera*, the restaurant Zane had turned him on to years earlier, was his typical watering hole. He'd feel important, rubbing elbows with the city's high-rollers, catching a nice buzz while handing out business cards to potential clients. However, given his drunkness, he didn't dare drive to the fancy Italian eatery.

Despite its lack of sophistication and affluent clientele, this dingy neighborhood bar still made Phil feel important. All eyes had been on him since he pulled up in his Mercedes and strolled in wearing his faux suit that looked much more expensive than it actually was. It was only midday, but the place was still hosting a dozen unrefined characters who mostly kept to themselves. They were the city's drunken dregs, all gathering to forget how miserable their lives had become by downing cheap swill to mask their pain.

Towards the back of the small, dimly lit bar, a tall, muscular man with his hair tied back in a ponytail and wearing a leather vest with some undecipherable lettering embroidered on its back bent over the location's only pool table and appeared to be practicing his eight-ball. His sizable arms were adorned with ink, and a toothpick rested in his expressionless mouth.

Phil made a mental note to keep his distance from the intimidating man who looked like he was part of some unsavory motorcycle gang. He averted his gaze to avoid upsetting the beast and spotted an old jukebox in the bar's far corner.

A brunette woman wearing a skimpy denim skirt stood with her back to him and seemed to be browsing the machine's selection of music. Her long legs rested comfortably in a pair of black cowboy boots, and her snug blue t-shirt was hiked up enough to show the small of her tattooed back. Phil hoped that her face would be as attractive as her backside when she turned around.

As he sipped his drink, his mind returned to his disastrous encounter with Jenna Parker in the break room of the marketing firm he'd help build. He'd drunkenly pushed things too far, and there would definitely be repercussions for his actions. He knew there was no way she wouldn't report the incident to Zane, and she'd likely spin it to paint herself as innocently as possible. She'd been flirting with him from the moment they met, acting coy while lustfully batting her big, brown eyes at him, but that's certainly not how she'd portray it to their boss.

No, she'd make Phil out to be the bad guy, just as his trifling secretary had done three years prior, and his neck would be on the chopping block once again. He hoped Zane would take the word of a man he'd known for five years, the same man who'd expanded his business tenfold, over that of a girl from the ghetto he'd known for only three months, but the love-struck Adonis hadn't been making the best decisions lately.

Realizing who Zane would end up siding with, he'd fled the building as quickly as possible under the guise of meeting with an important client. He needed time to come up with an explanation for the break room debacle, one that would hopefully save his job, but nothing was coming to mind. He'd have to deny Jenna's accusations, pit his word against hers, and hope for the best.

"That fuckin' whore," he muttered under his breath before gulping down the rest of his drink. He ordered one more, this time quietly so as not to upset the bartender, as the jukebox began to sound the easily discernible voice of Johnny Cash.

The woman who'd chosen the song finally turned and revealed her disappointingly weathered face. She took notice of Phil and flashed him a smile, and he returned it with his smile while politely raising his glass to her. He watched her hips sway as she walked across the room, her tight midriff exposed and her dark, curly hair falling around her shoulders.

She sat next to him at the bar, reeking of cigarettes and booze, her teeth heavily stained from years of partying taking precedence over hygiene. Phil was sure she'd have plenty of stories to tell if her mind wasn't too fried to remember them all. He guessed her age to be around forty, but it was hard to tell since her face looked as though it had been riding hard and put away wet. On the other hand, her body was undeniably attractive and still held an aura of youth.

"That your Mercedes outside?" she asked, nodding towards the parking lot.

"You know it," Phil flirtatiously grinned as he stole a glance at her cleavage. Her shirt was cut extremely low, and her ample breasts, shamelessly on display, were definitely piquing his interest.

"Look at you, all fancy," she giggled while playfully tugging the lapel of his suit jacket. Phil hadn't seen her order one, yet the bartender slid a bottle of Bud Light in front of the woman, telling him she was a regular in this seedy bar.

"That's me," he replied, pausing to sip his drink and then adding, "Mr. Fancy."

"You have a first name, Mr. Fancy, or should I just call you that?" the woman asked before throwing her head back and chugging half of her beer while an impressed Phil watched in awe.

"Name's… Zane," he answered with a smirk. "Zane Talbot."

He extended his hand, and she shook it while turning her head to release a low burp.

"Well," she sniffed, "my name's Amber, but you can call me whatever you want, honey."

She shot him a wink and finished the rest of her beer. Following her lead, Phil pounded the rest of his rum and Coke and signaled for the bartender to bring him yet another.

The face of his new drinking buddy was looking better with each passing second. Right now, at a time when he was feeling so bitterly dejected, her company was just what he needed. Even through his intoxication, he could tell she was a working girl, but that didn't bother him. He was just happy to have somebody by his side. Somebody who recognized his importance. Somebody who found him attractive, even if the flattery came with a price tag.

"Don't see guys like you in here very often, cutie," she commented as the bartender replaced her empty bottle with a full one. "You a lawyer or something?"

"I run my own marketing firm," Phil boasted, reaching into his breast pocket and pulling out one of Zane's business cards. He always kept several of them on him for occasions such as this.

"Damn, you're a big deal, huh?" she asked with wide, hazel eyes as she read the card and stuffed it into her bra.

"You could say that," he chuckled, his face beaming with pride.

"What are you doing in a place like this?" she questioned with her voice low to not offend the bartender or any patron who may overhear her. "Shouldn't you be at some country club or something?"

"All I do is hang out with rich people lately," Phil explained. "You know, celebrities, politicians, CEOs, Wall Street bigwigs. I felt like I was losing touch with the common man, you know? I saw this place and decided to pop in for a drink. Get back in touch with my roots and all that," he lied.

"Celebrities?" she asked in excitement, her face suddenly looking years younger as she lit up in delight. "Like who? Tell me!"

"I don't like to name drop," Phil began as he waved his hand dismissively. He leaned in close to her and whispered, "But I played eighteen holes last week with Ashton Kutcher."

"Shut up!" Amber burst, playfully shoving his shoulder. "You're lying!"

"I swear," Phil laughed, flashing her the Scout's Honor sign by raising three fingers to his brow. "I'm working on the new Nikon campaign, and he's a big part of it. We've actually gotten pretty close over the last few months. He's a perfect guy."

Amber hung on his every word, listening with a look of fascination and admiration as Phil, still posing as Zane Talbot, spun a series of elaborate lies. While he spoke, she sucked down another two beers, and by the time he finished walking her through the inner workings of the marketing firm he claimed was his, he'd polished off his third strong rum and Coke. He was now extremely drunk, his voice slurring heavily, and Amber, fully enamored with the man she believed to be somebody else, was just beginning to feel the buzz of the beers she'd slammed so quickly. She placed a nicotine-stained hand on Phil's cheek, leaned in close, and spoke softly into his ear.

"I'll suck your dick for forty bucks."

"Naughty girl," Phil replied in a quiet purr as he tried to focus on the woman that alcohol had transformed from tired and worn to youthful and beautiful. "What if I want you for the whole day?"

"The whole day, huh?" she giggled, placing a hand on his inner thigh and slowly moving it closer to his crotch. "Five hundred," she answered hushedly so their negotiation would stay between them.

"Three hundred and you have a deal," he fired back with a grin.

"Come on, don't be cheap," she sighed as her hand grazed his penis. "You're rich. You can afford it."

"Let's meet in the middle. Four hundred and I'll get our drinks for the rest of the day," Phil countered. Even this drunk, he wasn't going to let anyone hustle him.

"Will you grab my tab here, too?" she asked with a hopeful smile.

"Done," he nodded, trying not to fall off his stool as he reached into his back pocket to retrieve his wallet.

"You're a doll," she squealed and kissed him on the cheek. "I'm going to go have a quick smoke. I'll meet you outside."

"Be right—" covering his mouth with his fist, he let out a loud belch and finished his short sentence with, "Out."

He smacked her ass as she turned to head out the door, and once she'd stepped outside, he gestured for the bartender to ring him up.

"That'll be thirty-seven even," the burly, no-nonsense man told him as he glanced at the small pad of paper on which he'd been tallying their drinks. Phil fished two twenties out of his wallet and threw them down on the bar top.

"Keep the change," Phil told him smugly, rising from his seat and using the bar to steady himself.

"Wow, three bucks," the bartender replied sarcastically. "Should I invest that in gold or silver?"

"Gold," Phil answered hesitantly, so drunk he failed to pick up on the man's facetiousness.

"Tell you what," the irritated barkeep scowled, "maybe you should keep the three bucks. You're gonna have to buy quite a few rubbers if you plan on fucking that skank."

He nodded towards Amber, who stood puffing on a cigarette just outside the entrance. An old drunk seated at the end of the bar overheard their exchange and laughed at the bartender's joke.

"Maybe you should eat a bag of shit and mind your own fuckin' business," Phil rebutted loudly.

The tall, muscular man who'd been shooting pool heard this comment and immediately paused his practice. Standing up straight and looking quite menacing in doing so, he rested the bottom bumper of his cue on the floor while holding its tip with a big, strong hand. His eyes filled more with concern than anger, and he locked on to Phil first before moving on to the bartender.

"It's okay," the bartender silently mouthed to the hulking man, raising a hand to him in reassurance. Although he was staggeringly intoxicated, Phil could tell that these two were friends and simply looking out for each other.

"I'm sorry," Phil slurred apologetically. Reaching into his wallet, he pulled out another twenty and slapped it down on the bar top. "Thank you for the drinks."

"Just get home safe," the bartender replied, his anger melting into genuine compassion for the pudgy, downtrodden man standing before him in a cheap, knock-off suit.

"Want us to call you a cab?" the behemoth holding the pool cue stepped forward to ask in a deep, raspy voice.

"No, I'm good, but thanks, guys," Phil politely waved as he turned to leave, suddenly feeling guilty for his obnoxious behavior. He'd labeled these men miscreants based on their rough exteriors, but they'd proven to be kind, understanding people who genuinely cared about his well-being.

Stumbling his way outside, he reunited with Amber, who helped him make the short walk to his car. She refused to let him drive, ignoring his protests and insisting she take the wheel. He finally conceded and sank into the passenger seat while she hopped into the driver's side, thrilled at the chance to drive a Mercedes for the first time.

"Where's your place?" she asked as she carefully backed out of the parking lot.

"Far, far, away," Phil answered, fighting to keep his eyes open. "Just find a motel. I'll pay. I don't give a shit."

"Okay, babe. I know a place right down the street," she replied while she maneuvered the expensive vehicle.

"I bet you do," Phil muttered, laughing at his quip. He briefly nodded off, and when he awoke, he found them parked outside the lobby of *Travel Inn*, a cheap, rather disreputable motel just off of the interstate.

"Go check in," Amber instructed as the car sat idling by the motel's front entrance.

"Yes, ma'am," Phil answered, rubbing his eyes and pulling a pair of sunglasses from his glove compartment. He opened the passenger door and moved to exit the car, then paused in a moment of clarity. He turned and pulled his keys from the ignition, realizing the last thing he needed was for this prostitute to drive off with his five-month-old Mercedes.

"Really?" she scoffed as he slid the sunglasses on and stepped out of the car.

"Better safe than sorry," he grunted, then headed into the motel's small lobby, trying not to stumble. He returned moments later, dangling a pair of room keys, and handed his own keys back to Amber.

After his paid companion pulled the car into a parking space alongside the motel, he had her pop the trunk so he could retrieve the last rum-filled water bottle he'd stashed. He wasn't happy to learn that the room was on the second floor but made it up the flight of stairs without falling.

"I got us the penthouse suite," he joked while leading her into the small, outdated room with a queen-size bed draped with a rather ugly maroon comforter positioned in its center. Beside it, two worn chairs sat tucked into a little table, and he wasn't surprised to see the antiquated CRT television sitting atop a short bureau that looked like it had seen better days. He was surprised, however, to find a mini-fridge, capped with a microwave, standing to the side of the bureau. Both seemed in decent condition and were unexpected amenities for a room costing only forty dollars. The room looked like a vestige of the 1980s, but he didn't expect any less from a cheap motel that catered primarily to truckers and prostitutes.

Phil removed his suit jacket, tossed it onto one of the two chairs, and unbuttoned his shirt while Amber entered the bathroom. He could hear the sink running and hoped she was freshening up with a quick whore's bath.

Clumsily kicking off his shoes, he slid his pants down with one hand while the other clung to the table in an effort to stabilize himself. When he spotted the bottle of disguised alcohol he'd set on the bureau by his sunglasses, he stumbled over to it, took a large gulp without a wince, and then drifted back to the bed.

Using a clever move he'd familiarized himself with in recent months. He hid his wallet, cell phone, and keys in his pillowcase to protect himself from theft should he pass out. The disoriented drunk peeled back its dated comforter and climbed in, surprised by how comfortable the mattress was, and closed his eyes to the spinning room. He was on the verge of passing out when Amber startled him awake by slinking into bed next to him, and he could smell that her attempt to wash up hadn't accomplished much.

"We gonna play, or you just wanna sleep?" she smiled as she seductively licked the tip of her index finger.

"Take this off," Phil groggily commanded, tugging on her shirt.

"Whatever you want, baby," she smirked. Doing as instructed, she sat up and peeled her tight blue t-shirt off.

"This, too," he insisted, pointing at her white bra.

"I like a man who knows what he wants," she giggled. Reaching behind her back, she unhooked it as told. Her breasts, quite large for her small frame, were still perky and every bit as spectacular as Phil had imagined.

"Goddamn, those are nice," Phil commented as he ran the back of his fingers over her hardening right nipple. "They real?"

"All natural, baby," she answered, climbing between his legs and beginning to rub his cock through his red boxers. "You like that? "She teased while looking up at him with hazel eyes, their corners marked with premature wrinkles from her rough life.

"Mmhmm," he groaned as she pulled his boxers down and took his flaccid member in her hand, gently stroking it up and down while he felt her warm breath on its tip. He wasn't surprised when she lowered her head and took him in her mouth without pausing to at least consider using a condom. Amber, if that was her real name, didn't look like she made cleanliness or sexual safety much of a priority.

After ten minutes of mouthing his soft, unimpressive cock, Amber began showing signs of agitation at Phil's inability to get aroused. She let out a long, irritated sigh, then continued to suck his limp penis as he watched her with droopy, inebriated eyes. After another five minutes, she couldn't contain her frustration any longer and had to say something.

"You gonna be able to get hard, or what?"

"Yeah, sorry. Just the booze. Don't stop," Phil replied, placing his hand on the back of her head and moving it back down to his lackluster manhood.

She was about to call it quits and give her aching jaw a rest when Phil's cock finally began to show signs of life. Five minutes later, he was erect enough for her to climb on top, but he stopped her to insist they use protection. Proving to be a true professional, she pulled a condom out of the back pocket of her denim skirt. She hurriedly tore the package open, wrapping the prophylactic over his hard member before it had time to go limp again. She hiked her skirt up, revealing she wasn't wearing any panties, and positioned herself over his shaft. Reaching down, she guided him inside her unkempt vagina and slowly gyrated her hips as his sweaty hands gripped her outer thighs.

"There we go, baby," she smiled, covering his hands with her own and clenching them tightly as her body began to rock back and forth.

"Take that cock, you dirty whore," he breathed. His eyes closed in concentration, and his hips thrust up and down.

"Yeah? Am I your little slut?" she moaned, playing along with his apparent appetite for degradation.

"You're fucking right you are, you bitch," he growled, his face twisting in coital focus as his cock slid in and out of her wet hole. His hands broke free of hers and moved to her firm ass, squeezing it hard and using it to control their rhythm.

"Shit," she cursed when he slipped out of her. She tried fitting him back in, but he'd started to go limp again, and she couldn't get him inside. "Maybe you should sober up some first?"

"No, I'm good," Phil assured her, pulling her onto the bed beside him and sliding his boxers off. Now wearing only his black dress socks and a loose condom, he gracelessly rose to his knees and squeezed his hairy body between her spread legs, seemingly unashamed of his sagging chest and large, flabby belly. Focusing on her large breasts, he began jerking his deflating cock in an attempt to revive his erection.

"That's it, stroke that dick for me, baby," Amber whispered as she watched him frantically tug himself.

Two minutes later, when he'd resuscitated his hard-on, he placed her legs on his shoulders and sank all five inches of his stiff member inside her, grunting as he began drunkenly pumping away.

"Give me that big cock!" she exaggeratedly cried out, stroking his ego as Phil repeatedly pounded into her.

"Take it, you whore!" he grunted, his eyes closed and sweat forming on his brow. "Take it, Jenna, you ghetto whore!"

"Yes, that's right, I'm Jenna! Fuck me! Fuck me!" Amber moaned, showcasing her acting chops by transforming into whatever girl John was fantasizing about as he flailed around between her legs.

"You take it, Jenna, you fucking slut!" he snarled. Opening his eyes, Phil watched all four of her breasts bouncing on her two chests. He was seeing double, the motion making him nauseous, and the alcohol was killing his erection yet again.

"Jesus Christ," she muttered in annoyance as he slipped out of her for a second time.

"I'm not paying you for your fucking commentary!" Phil suddenly burst, violently slapping her across her face with the back of his hand.

"Ow! What the fuck?" she screamed, throwing her hands up to shield herself.

"You fucking bitch!" he snapped, reaching down and wrapping his hands around her throat. *"You think you're better than me? You think you can get me fired, you cunt?"*

Amber was long gone, replaced in his mind by Jenna Parker, the woman who'd made a mockery of him and, in all likeliness, had cost him his job. He tightened his grip on her neck, choking the life out of her as her face turned bright red. She fought for air beneath him, clawing at his hands desperately to break free, but she was no match for the weight he had pressed down on her.

The face that had seemed so friendly only an hour earlier at the bar was now unrecognizable filled with a hatred she feared murderous. His teeth were gritted, his brow furrowed in anger, and his eyes were dark and cold.

Amber's legs flailed and her body twisted as she struggled to save herself, her heart thudding and mind racing in panic as his grip tightened again. He was raving like a madman, spittle coating her face as he yelled, but she was unable to make out his words.

She pounded at his face, but the blows didn't seem to faze him, and when she tried scratching it, he pulled out of reach. She prayed somebody would hear the altercation and rescue her, but she could feel the life slipping out of her and knew they'd never make it in time. Reaching behind her head, she pulled the pillow out from under her curly hair and futilely hit him in the face with it. It made no impact, falling to the floor by the side of the bed, and she was seconds away from losing consciousness when her left outstretched arm felt a blunt, heavy object. Her fingertips stretched to reach it, and at the last moment, they succeeded in doing so. She quickly swung it into the side of his head with all of her remaining strength, and he immediately fell onto his side, knocked out cold by whatever she'd driven into him.

With her chest heaving and oxygen returning to her brain, she realized the telephone on the motel's nightstand had just saved her life. The corner of it was marked with red, and when she managed to crawl out from under the man she still assumed was Zane Talbot, she saw that his head was gushing blood. She didn't know if he was alive or dead but didn't plan on sticking around long enough to find out. She was still regaining her breath, her pulse racing as she scanned the room and retraced her steps.

While Phil's bloodstain spread across the bed's white sheets, she drew the curtains closed tightly, placed the "do not disturb" sign on the door, and wiped the room free of her fingerprints. His body showed no signs of life as she carefully peeled the condom from his penis and flushed it down the toilet, which she hoped would also erase her DNA from the room.

When her foot accidentally grazed the pillow that had fallen onto the floor, she noticed an odd lump that, upon investigation, turned out to be his wallet, cell phone, and car keys. She'd searched for them earlier, rooting through his pants and jacket, but had found only a handful of business cards that she chose to simply shove into her back pocket instead of wiping free of her fingerprints.

For the next four hours, Amber sat shaking on the corner of the bed, sobbing quietly and occasionally glancing at his motionless body. She'd struck him hard just above his right temple, and the sheets were drenched in blood.

She was fairly certain he was dead and reminded herself that she'd acted strictly in self-defense. Thumbing through his wallet, she quickly pieced together that he'd been lying about his name and shook her head at her own gullibility. Finally, when darkness had fallen, she slid his sunglasses on, covered her face with her curly hair, and fled the motel undetected, leaving Phil Miller's body in a pool of drying blood.

Chapter Thirteen

"Still no word from Phil?" Jenna asked as she poked her head into Zane's office. Five days had passed since Phil Miller's mysterious disappearance, and the firm was abuzz with rumors and speculation. Some believed he'd met with foul play, while others suggested suicide. A few thought he'd snapped and driven to Mexico to start a new life, and those aware of his drinking problem assumed he was on an epic bender.

"Nothing," Zane sighed, standing before his large flat-screen television, reviewing artwork for a client's new campaign.

Phil's cell phone had been going straight to voicemail for days, indicating that it had either been broken or purposely shut off. When Phil Miller worked for Enterprise Marketing, his attendance record had been fairly impressive, even amid the debacle with his secretary three years prior. In the rare instances when he did miss work, he'd always call in with his sincerest apologies. This absence was unlike Phil, but neither Zane nor Jenna were overly concerned. They both assumed he'd vanished in shame, an unspoken resignation after his inappropriate exchange with

Jenna five days earlier. It seemed likely that he feared termination and left quietly of his own volition. Still, Zane had left him several voice and text messages along with a handful of e-mails, all of which had gone unanswered, and had even driven to his house on two separate occasions in hopes of resolving things with his protégé.

The staff was unaware of the embarrassing events leading up to Phil's abrupt departure, and Zane intended to keep it that way. He planned to announce Phil's retirement from the company at the end of the work day, omitting the man's transgressions and would begin searching for his replacement the following week.

"I guess that's that then, huh?" Jenna asked as she stepped into the office and closed the door behind her.

"That's that," Zane agreed, turning to accept her kiss with a smile. "I officially need a new right-hand man."

"Can you make it a right-hand woman?" Jenna joked. "That way, we don't have a repeat of Phil?"

"That's not a bad idea," Zane nodded while using the remote he was holding to shut the television off.

"You know I'd love to have you fill his shoes, but I don't see that going over well with everyone."

"I totally understand, baby," she grinned as he wrapped his arms around her and pulled her into him for another kiss. "You don't need to explain it again."

There were already enough rumors of favoritism floating around, and she was well aware of the volatile reaction he'd face if he promoted her to Phil's position instead of selecting somebody with more experience. She belonged in the art department where her true talent could shine, and she was at her happiest. Soliciting new clients and managing accounts was a job she had no interest in anyhow.

"Lunch?" he asked while he playfully squeezed her ass.

"Lunch," she giggled as she straightened his tie for him.

Over the three months she'd worked with the firm, they'd tried to coordinate their lunch breaks as often as they could. The timing didn't always work out, but when it did, they had fun exploring local restaurants together.

"Opa?" he questioned, flashing his perfect smile.

"Opa," she agreed. They'd discovered the small Greek diner a month earlier and had both enjoyed it enough to add it to their rotation.

Zane walked Jenna, her purse slung over her shoulder, out of his office, and the two politely nodded at his secretary as they left the small reception area. They'd just stepped into the long, wide hallway that led toward the elevators when a stir from the art department roused their curiosity.

Peeking in to identify the source of the fuss, they both froze mouths agape in shocked disbelief at the sight of Phil Miller. His head was wrapped in a thick bandage, his left eye was blackened, and he stood with several employees excitedly huddled around him as his boisterous voice recounted the horrible tragedy that had befallen him. His story stopped mid-sentence as he spotted Zane and Jenna in the doorway and motioned for them to be part of his captivated audience. Despite his battered appearance, he was beaming with a large, somehow unsettling smile as he waved them into the room. They joined the semicircle that had formed around him, their faces clearly stunned by his unexpected presence.

"Did you hear what happened?" he asked them with the same out-of-place smile as he pointed at his black eye.

"My God…" Zane muttered in bewilderment while staring at the medical gauze circling Phil's head. Jenna stood close to him, her face stunned, unable to pry her eyes off Phil's beaten exterior.

"I got carjacked!" Phil cackled loudly. "They whacked me in the head with a bat or something. Stole my car and took my wallet and cell phone, too," he expounded.

"Jesus…" Jenna gasped, cupping her hands over her mouth in horror.

"Right?" Phil nodded. "I don't remember much. Somebody found me on the side of the road and called 911. All I know is that I woke up in the hospital yesterday afternoon. Apparently, I'd been in a damn coma for three days," he lied. He certainly couldn't tell them, or anybody for that matter, what had really transpired. When he'd failed to check out of the motel on time, management had let themselves into his room after their calls had gone unanswered. They'd found his unresponsive body slumped over in a pool of blood and immediately called an ambulance and the police.

"I'm so sorry," Zane replied empathetically. "Did you see who did it?"

"Did they catch them?" Jenna chimed in before Phil had a chance to respond.

"Is there a police report?" Zane quickly added to the growing list of questions.

"Whoa!" Phil chuckled as he threw up his hands and gestured for them to slow down. "I don't really remember much. I think a couple of Mexican guys, but the cops don't have any leads yet. They just filed my report this morning before I was discharged from the hospital."

He wasn't lying about the latter part of his answer. He really had spent three days in a coma, and the police had taken his statement shortly before he was released three hours earlier. He'd told them he'd made the mistake of leaving his door ajar to get some fresh air and that two Latino men had barged in and assaulted him.

"You seem to be taking this quite well," Zane couldn't help but notice. Jenna glanced at him, then looked at Phil with a hint of skepticism, unsure if she believed his story.

"Hey, what else can I do?" Phil sighed. "I have ten stitches in my cracked skull, and somebody's out there driving my car around. Thankfully, I have good insurance! Oh, and I wasn't able to cancel my credit card until yesterday since I was goddamn unconscious, and in the three days I was out of it, they managed to rack up thousands of dollars in charges. My bank's fraud department is looking into it, and we're hoping they can turn up some leads. I can do nothing at this point except wait and hope they catch the bastards. I'm just trying to stay positive right now. They say laughter's the best medicine, right?"

Most of his short rant wasn't a lie. When he'd finally regained consciousness, he'd used the phone in his hospital room to cancel his credit card and found that Amber had already been spending his money quite liberally. His insurance company had sprung for a rental car, and the police were watching for his Mercedes.

"You're so lucky you're alive, you poor thing!" Leeza, one of the firm's most respected artists, commented with her hand placed over her heart in sympathy.

"I know," Phil agreed. "The police didn't contact you?" he nervously asked, turning his attention back to his boss.

"No, not at all," Zane shrugged.

"Tucson's finest," Phil snorted. "I figured they'd at least shoot you a call."

"I haven't heard a thing from anyone. I tried reaching you, but you just vanished," Zane explained. Losing interest, the staff dispersed to their workstations and resumed their work.

"So you had no idea where I was?" Phil questioned, relieved that the authorities hadn't contacted his boss. He hoped it would stay that way since an investigation would undoubtedly unravel his bogus story. The last thing he needed was anyone finding out he'd been brained with a telephone in a cheap motel room, his blood alcohol level through the roof when he was supposed to meet with a client.

"We'd just assumed you'd…" Zane trailed off as he and Jenna shot each other a look.

"Assumed what? That I'd quit?" Phil finished for him.

"Well, yeah," Zane replied.

"And not given any notice whatsoever?" Phil scoffed at the absurdity of this notion.

"Well, yeah," Jenna echoed.

"Come on, you know I'd never do that," Phil incredulously shot back.

"I think we should finish this conversation in my office," Zane leaned in slightly and whispered through his teeth, maintaining a smile so as not to evoke any suspicion or concern from his employees. A look of worry crossed Phil's bruised face as he feared what was to come. Jenna followed behind them as they headed back into Zane's private lair, his secretary gasping at the sight of Phil's wounds as they passed her.

With the door closed behind them, Zane took a seat behind his desk and invited Phil to choose from one of the two chairs positioned in front of it. He slowly sank into one while Jenna stood by Zane's side instead of taking the other. For a fleeting moment, she felt sorry for Phil, looking battered and broken, his life in shambles yet trying his best to appear unshaken.

"After the stunt you pulled with Jenna a few days ago," Zane began after clearing his throat, "we assumed you'd terminated your relationship with the company."

"I'm not sure I follow," Phil replied with a look of confusion.

"Oh, please!" Jenna blurted angrily. "You know you—"

"Jenna," Zane interrupted her with a raised hand. He straightened his tie, rolled his chair closer to his desk, and folded his hands across its oak surface. "It's come to my attention that you may have made some inappropriate comments to Jenna here just before your disappearance."

"I... I have no recollection of that," Phil gulped. "Ever since the attack, my memory's been kind of screwy."

"I see," Zane replied. Beside him, he could feel Jenna seething angrily at Phil's poorly feigned memory lapse.

"Jenna, if I said or did anything to offend you, I sincerely apologize," Phil addressed her pleadingly. He looked back at Zane and continued, "You know how I am. Sometimes, I joke around and take things a bit too far. I'm really sorry. I'm sure I didn't mean anything by it, and I promise you it won't happen again."

"You're so full of shit!" Jenna hissed. Once again, Zane silenced her by raising his hand.

"Look, Phil, you've done a lot for this company over the years. Nobody's denying that," Zane spoke calmly. "I'd like us to resolve this amicably. I'm willing to keep you on board here, but there will be some changes."

"Okay..." Phil responded cautiously. He'd stepped into the office under the assumption he'd be getting fired, and although he was surprised to hear he still had a job, he knew the stipulations for his continued employment weren't going to be good.

"I'm pulling you off the BMW campaign. Jenna's going to oversee it from here on out," Zane told him firmly.

"What?" an outraged Phil spat. "You can't do that! That's my account!"

"Relax," Zane insisted, "it's still your account. I'm just pulling you from it until their new campaign is finished. Jenna's going to present it to them on Wednesday. If they like it, her work will be done, and you can retake the reins."

"Jenna's going to present it?" Phil looked at her with doubt, and she flashed him a look of smug satisfaction. He returned his sunken eyes to Zane and mumbled, "I'm always doing the presenting…"

"After you vanished, we had to develop a Plan B," Zane explained. "Jenna knows more about their new campaign than anybody, and I have faith in her ability to sell it to them."

"But I'm back now!" Phil bleated, his eyes now wide and full of desperation. "I can present!"

"The presentation's in two days, and you look like you got hit by a truck," Zane pointed out, and after a brief pause, added, "No offense."

"Okay…" Phil sighed in defeat. He knew Zane was right and that he'd only hurt the campaign they'd worked so hard on if he attempted to present the new marketing strategy in his current condition.

"Jenna, can you give us a few moments alone?" Zane asked as he turned his chair and looked up at her with a polite smile.

"Are you sure?" she muttered in concern.

"Yes, I just need a few minutes," he replied while Phil studied their short exchange. "Wait for me in the studio. I'll be in shortly."

Zane watched her exit the room, quietly closing the door behind her, as Phil sat with his right leg anxiously bouncing up and down. He was nervous and knew he had every right to be.

"Phil, I'm going to be blunt here," Zane began as he rose from his leather chair and gazed out the window. "As I said, you've done a lot for this company, and I appreciate it more than you know. The amount of business you've brought in is why I haven't tossed you out of here."

"Thank you," Phil replied meekly as he hung his head in shame.

"The main reason I'm pulling you from the BMW account is because I don't want you around, Jenna. Not now. Not ever," Zane's voice dropped to a growl as he turned to face the stout, balding man he once considered a valued confidant.

"Look, buddy, I don't know what she told you, but I can assure you I never—"

"Stop!" Zane's thunderous voice erupted, the sound of his large hands slapping down loudly on his desk causing Phil to recoil in fear. Suddenly filled with anger, his blue eyes locked onto his frightened protégé. "Just stop it. How stupid do you think I am? We both know you screwed up. It's written all over your face. You know Jenna wanted me to fire your ass, but I talked her down? She finally agreed to let things slide as long as she never has to deal with you again. From here on out, you're going to avoid her at all costs, you understand me?"

"Yeah…" a visibly shaken Phil agreed. "Yeah, I understand." He'd never seen Zane come anywhere close to losing his composure like this.

"Good," Zane glared. Clearing his throat and adjusting his suit jacket, he quickly regained his calm and spoke calmly. "You so much as speak one word to her, and you're done, got it?"

"I read you loud and clear," Phil assured, still trembling from Zane's brief explosion.

"And you're not out of the hot seat yet," Zane continued, remembering why he'd wanted to speak with Phil five days earlier.

Phil swallowed hard and replied, "What do you mean?"

"Whatever happened to those accounts I told you to look into? The missing funds? Ali told me you never spoke to her about it," Zane questioned. He began pacing by the large window with his hands behind his back.

"What?" Phil chimed indignantly. "I sure did! It was a few weeks ago, so I'm sure she just forgot."

"I see," Zane replied dubiously. He knew how busy Ali kept, but it wasn't in her fastidious nature to forget such a meaningful conversation. "If I recall, they were your accounts. How did you manage to misplace those expense reports? More importantly, how have you not found them by now?"

"Everything's accounted for, I guarantee that," Phil insisted. "I've been so busy with the BMW account, I've been bringing work home with me. All the expenses are at my place somewhere, don't worry about it.

"Don't worry about it?" Zane asked in irritation. "It's a lot of money that's unaccounted for. It's my job to worry about it."

"Right, you're absolutely right," Phil backpedaled. "I'll get those reports to you by the end of the week."

"I want to see every receipt," Zane demanded. He stopped pacing and studied Phil's tense face.

"Got it," Phil nodded while avoiding eye contact, uncomfortable with his boss's icy stare.

"You're dismissed," Zane said as he nodded toward the office door. He thought he heard Phil breathe a faint sigh of relief.

"Thank you," Phil forced a smile as he rose from the chair. He was typically a smooth talker, a trait he used to lure in clients, but he was also nervous. When placed in an uncomfortable situation, he'd speak excessively and had a tendency to volunteer too much information. As he backed his way towards the office door, again apologizing for his behavior and absence, his overactive mouth made a critical mistake by adding, "Kroger, Tanque Verde Ranch, and Hotel Congress, right? I'll get you their expenses by the end of the week."

He'd just turned to exit the room, his hand on the door's knob, when Zane's imposing voice stopped him.

"Wait!"

Phil froze in place for a moment before slowly facing his boss.

"Yes?" he asked with worry.

"I only told you about Kroger and Tanque Verde Ranch. How did you know about Hotel Congress?" Zane asked as he crossed the room and stood intimidatingly close to the man.

"I... I..." Phil stammered, his mind frantically searching for an excuse but only coming up with, "Ali told me."

"I don't think so," Zane shook his head. "I told her to keep that one strictly between me and her. And you just told me you haven't spoken to her in weeks. Try again."

"I... I..." Phil stammered again as guilt spread across his face. "I must have run into her at some point. This damn injury," he gulped as he pointed to the bandage wrapped around his head, "has my mind all jumbled."

"You're lying," Zane replied while shaking his head. "You're a great salesman, yet somehow, you're a terrible liar."

"I don't know what you're talking about," Phil laughed nervously.

"What did you do, Phil?" Zane questioned in disappointment.

"What do you mean?" Phil answered as his face flushed and beads of sweat began to form on his forehead just below the medical gauze.

"You took the money, didn't you?" Zane asked bluntly.

"What?" Phil scoffed. "Don't be ridiculous."

"Why did you do it?" Zane's face turned from anger to hurt at the realization that the man he once considered a trusted ally had betrayed him.

"You're crazy," Phil looked away in shame.

"Just tell me why," Zane persisted, his voice low and his blue eyes filled with deep sorrow.

"It's that little hood rat girlfriend of yours!" Phil suddenly burst into a rage. "She's poisoning your mind! Running around here like she owns the place, that bitch!"

"Choose your words," Zane warned in a furious growl, a finger pointed in Phil's face and his brow lowered in anger.

"You know she hits on me all the time, right?" Phil chuckled with a snort, still averting Zane's gaze by keeping his eyes locked onto the blank television screen mounted to the office wall.

"No, she doesn't, Phil," Zane fired back in disgust.

"She's been making eyes at me since day one!" Phil persisted.

"No, she hasn't," Zane laughed in amusement at Phil's desperate allegations.

"It's true!" Phil maintained, "And now she's trying to play us against each other."

"Phil, I know you did it. I just want to know why. I think I deserve that. I've treated you so well—"

"You've treated me so well?" Phil exploded, his face twisting in rage and his eyes, now fueled with contempt, no longer afraid to make contact with Zane's. "That's bullshit, and you know it! How have you treated me well, huh? By siding with that whore secretary over me?"

"Ah, so that's what this is about," Zane sighed, unfazed by Phil's maniacal look. The man had clearly come unhinged, but Zane showed no signs of fear.

"You're goddamn right. That's what this is about!" Phil screamed so loudly Zane was sure the entire firm could hear it. His face was now beet red, and what showed of his forehead was pulsing with pronounced veins. "You took her word over mine, then had the nerve to dock my pay twenty grand a year?"

"Yes, for five years, to cover the check I had to write her," Zane reminded him, realizing the math added up to the same amount of money his company was missing. It all made sense now. The three businesses in question weren't real clients, and there were no expense reports because Phil had simply pocketed the money. He might have gotten away with it had he taken the time to forge a list of receipts, but in his arrogance, he'd assumed everyone was too stupid to catch on.

"That's horse shit!" Phil barked. "That was my money, and I never touched that slut!"

"So you decided to, what, just steal that money back?" Zane asked in puzzlement.

"I didn't steal it. I earned it!" Phil defended through gritted teeth. Zane sensed the man wanted to take a swing at him but knew he was physically outmatched.

"Look, I'm not going to press charges," Zane sighed. "I'm not even going to take you to court. Just consider the money you stole your severance pay and get out."

"You can't do this to me!" Phil sneered. "You need me! I helped make this company what it is!"

"Your problem's always been thinking you weren't replaceable," Zane told him, disheartened by the man he'd hired years earlier and had such high hopes for. "Grab your things from your office and get out."

"Please, don't do this," Phil pleaded, the anger on his face turning to desperate panic. "I'll pay back the money. I'll—"

"Don't," Zane stopped him by first holding up his palm and then pointing at the door. "Just go."

His battered head lowered in defeat. Phil slowly opened the office door and stepped into the small reception area. Several employees who'd been drawn by the sound of his screaming voice were lingering there and hurried back to their designated departments. Knowing he had nothing of importance in his office, Phil slunk down the long, wide hallway, and Zane trailed behind him to see him out of the building. He called for the elevator, and when the doors parted, he entered and turned to face his former boss. With a forced smile and his eyes welling with tears, he sniffled, turned his hands into imaginary guns, and gave Zane one final, "Pow, pow!"

The gesture pulled at Zane's heartstrings and brought him back to when he'd hired Phil, still very much a kid then, fresh out of college. He returned his smile with a sincere one of his own, truly saddened to be parting on such unfortunate terms, and waved goodbye as the elevator doors closed.

Chapter Fourteen

"What the hell happened?" Jenna asked as she rushed down the hallway and met Zane standing outside the elevators in the main reception area of *Enterprise Marketing*. Debbie, the portly redhead who served as the firm's head secretary, sat behind the high counter, trying rather poorly to mind her own business.

Jenna understood her curiosity and was equally interested in discovering what had happened. She'd left Zane's office under the pretense that things were working themselves out, and minutes later, World War III had erupted.

"It's a long story," an exasperated Zane told her. "Let's just say Phil Miller won't be with us anymore."

"Mr. Miller's gone?" Debbie chimed in, unable to contain herself any longer.

"Unfortunately, it appears so," Zane answered her with a polite grin.

"That's too bad," she replied somberly. "I really liked him."

Jenna rolled her eyes but kept her comments to herself.

"Seriously, what happened?" she leaned in and asked him again quietly. "Everybody's talking…"

"I'll tell you over dinner," he promised as he led her into the hallway and out of earshot from Debbie. "I fired Phil," he spoke softly so as not to be overheard, then glanced at his watch. "There's no way I can do lunch right now, babe. I'm sorry. I have a ton of things I need to handle."

"I completely understand," Jenna nodded. "Go do your thing. I'll grab you something while I'm out and drop it by your office shortly."

"You're an angel," he smiled, stealing a quick kiss after glancing down the hallway to make sure there were no onlookers.

"I know," she joked as they started down the hall together.

"Primavera tonight?" he asked. They came to a stop just outside the art department so she could grab the purse she'd set down at her workstation. The Italian restaurant had also become her favorite, but they hadn't visited it in two weeks.

"Only if I get to pay this time," she teased, knowing he'd never actually allow her to pick up the check.

"Yeah, no," he laughed. "Tell you what..." he whispered, "how about you cut out early today? Take off at three, swing home, and get all dolled up. I should be out of here by five. I'll make a reservation for six."

"Perfect," she beamed. "I can't wait to hear about Phil!"

"I have some more news for you, too. Good news," he playfully winked. He headed to his office, leaving her to wonder what had happened with Phil and what the good news would be. She had some news she'd yet to share with him but wasn't sure if he'd consider it good news.

Two days earlier, she'd passed on having lunch with him in favor of visiting an obstetrician she'd set up an appointment with. She learned that the baby was healthy, and the doctor confirmed what she'd suspected: she was three months along, and the child had likely been conceived the first night they'd slept together.

After leaving the obstetrician's office, she'd sat pensively in her car for nearly ten minutes before phoning the clinic they'd referred her to and scheduling a visit for the following week. She was surprised by how attached she'd grown to her baby in the few short days since learning of her pregnancy and was undecided whether or not she'd go through with the abortion.

Tonight, she would tell Zane about the pregnancy, and his reaction would determine the course she'd choose. She'd wanted to tell him earlier in the week, but Phil's mysterious disappearance had made things stressful enough. She didn't want to add to that stress by springing a baby on her overworked and overwhelmed lover and opted to hold out until the issue with Phil had been resolved. Now that it apparently had been, she couldn't keep the truth from him any longer. She had to tell Zane about the baby tonight.

Grabbing her purse, she headed down to the building's lobby and surveyed the parking lot for any sign of Phil. Satisfied that he was truly gone, she hurried to her car and drove towards *Opa*, calling the Greek restaurant to place a takeout order.

As promised, she returned with his lunch and found him hunched over his desk amidst a sea of paperwork. He paused long enough to thank her with a smile and a kiss, and she left him to finish his business. She ate her own lunch in the break room while chatting with a coworker from the art department but kept glancing at the door, fearing Phil would appear at any second. She had to remind herself that he was gone, this time for good and was no longer a threat. She'd been dreaming of this day for three months, and now that it had become a reality, it seemed almost surreal.

When three o'clock rolled around, she took Zane up on his offer by leaving early to head back to the lavish adobe estate she'd been calling home. There, she showered and slipped into the elegant red evening dress he'd generously surprised her with the month before, and as she sat doing her make-up first and hair second, she practiced the ways she might tell him about their baby.

Whatever approach she chose, she knew him well enough to know he'd be supportive. Still, a small doubt lingered in the back of her overactive mind and filled her with dread. What if he wasn't as receptive to the news as she'd hoped?

She'd already decided that if he showed even the slightest inkling of disappointment, she'd go through with the scheduled abortion that was only six days away. She'd become quite good at reading him and would know if he was faking joy. If he showed genuine excitement, she'd cancel the appointment and become a mother much earlier in life than she'd anticipated.

At 5:26 p.m., she heard the familiar sound of Zane's town car, and he strolled through the large oak doors of his impressive dwelling moments later.

She'd been anxiously waiting for him on the living room's impressive suede sofa, pretending to read a magazine in an attempt to act as casually as possible. She knew he was every bit as good at reading her as she was at reading him and hoped he wouldn't sense her nervous energy. She was dying to hear what happened with Phil and equally curious about his supposedly good news, but breaking her pregnancy to him was filling her with more apprehension than she had thought it would.

"Wow!" he exclaimed with a smile as he strolled into the living room. "You look amazing!"

"Thank you," she blushed, tossing the magazine back on the marble coffee table and rising to take his extended hand.

"You ready to go?" he asked, giving her a quick peck on the cheek so as not to mess up the red lipstick that matched her beautiful dress.

"I've been ready," she answered with a grin. "I can't take this suspense! You have to tell me all about Phil," she insisted.

"Patience, dear, patience," he chuckled as he guided her to the waiting town car, stopping to set the estate's alarm system before Carl chauffeured them to *Primavera*.

As the car zigzagged its way across town, Zane finally divulged his reason for terminating Phil, and Jenna listened in shock as he revealed the extent of the man's betrayal. To do so meant offering full disclosure by admitting that his firm had been missing much money, but he couldn't hide it from her any longer.

She was stunned by both the amount and how brazen Phil had been in his theft, but she was even more surprised by his poor attempt to cover his tracks. She knew the guy was a scumbag, but she'd always considered him intelligent. Apparently, they'd both overestimated his wit.

Jenna was still reeling from the startling circumstances of Phil's departure as the car delivered them out front of their favorite Italian eatery. Despite the unfortunate events regarding Phil, Zane assured her that he still had some very good news he'd be sharing as they enjoyed their dinner. Jenna announced that she had some news of her own, an admission that piqued Zane's interest, and would also be sharing it over their meal.

Seated at the recessed table Zane had reserved, Jenna flipped through the menu with her mind, returning to their magical first date here in this very restaurant. The place had a special hold on her heart thanks to that magnificent evening, and whenever they returned, she was reminded of that perfect outing.

Every time they came back, she'd try something new, and tonight, she settled on the gnocchi di ricotta while Zane stuck to his favorite pollo alla cacciatore. She tried to pry his news out of him while they waited for their meals to arrive, but he remained tight-lipped and spilled nothing. He tried to do the same, prodding her to share her news, but fearing ruining their dinner, she resolved to tell him over dessert. He joked that her news already sounded sweet, and she couldn't help but laugh at his ridiculous quip. His ability to make her laugh, even when she was feeling down, was something she loved about him.

Zane was slightly taken aback when Jenna refused her usual glass of wine, ordering a glass of milk in its place, but thankfully, he didn't question the change. Phil's deceit was the topic of conversation throughout most of their meal, and Zane had barely finished his last bite when Jenna began playfully badgering him about the good news he'd been holding so close to his vest.

"Okay, okay," he laughed, "I've kept you waiting long enough." He pushed his plate aside and leaned in close, a smirk spreading across his face as he unveiled his secret. "We're setting up an office in New York City. The transition starts next week."

"Wow!" Jenna replied, trying her best to sound enthused but feeling like she'd fallen short. "That's… that's… so soon!"

"I know," Zane glowed with pride. "I've been ironing out the details all week. The company's doing great, so it's time we finally expand to the East Coast."

"I'm so happy for you," Jenna lied, her heart sinking as Zane continued.

"I found a way to make it all work, even with the missing money Phil stole. We'll have to pinch some pennies, and things will be tight for a while, but we can do this. I'm sure of it."

"You weren't kidding when you said you had good news!" Jenna labored to smile, fighting hard to stay strong but quickly losing the battle and succumbing to her emotions. Her eyes began to well with tears of sorrow, but she was relieved when Zane mistook them for tears of joy.

"I knew you'd be happy," he beamed as Jenna dabbed her eyes with her napkin. "I managed to find some reasonable office space we can lease, and I'm flying to New York next week to check it out. If I don't snatch it up, somebody else will, and I don't want to pass it up. It's finally happening!" he paused to clap his hands together in exuberance. "We're joining the big boys on Madison Avenue!"

"I'm... I'm thrilled," she quietly sobbed while maintaining her strained smile. She knew he'd been wanting to launch a Northeast division but hadn't expected it to happen so soon. He was clearly elated by his announcement, grinning wide, his blue eyes alive with excitement, but she couldn't match his enthusiasm. Inside, she was devastated, her worst fear realized at dropping this unexpected bombshell. There was no way she could tell him about her pregnancy now. Not when he was so pleased, and rightfully so, with his accomplishment. Word of a baby would undoubtedly crush his spirits. She knew he was such a good man that he'd postpone his plans to see her through the pregnancy, but that would mean he'd have to pass up the office space he'd found, and she feared he might resent her for delaying the growth of his firm.

"I'll have to bring some new faces on board, but it shouldn't be hard finding people in New York City," Zane explained as he finished his wine and poured himself another celebratory glass. "I'll find somebody to take Phil's place here, and I'll have to oversee the Manhattan office for a few months."

"Oh, so you'll be staying in New York?" Jenna asked as she blotted her eyes once more and regained her composure.

"Well, I was hoping you'd come with me," he grinned hopefully. "I mean, I know your mom and brother are there. I figured it would give you a chance to see them again. Plus, I'd be honored if you'd introduce me to them."

"I'd love to see them again, but..." Jenna trailed off with a sigh.

"You don't have to see your old neighborhood, I promise," Zane assured her as he reached across the table to hold her hand.

"Thank you," she smiled, this time with sincerity. Four years had passed since she'd seen her two remaining family members, and as much as she missed them, the thought of stepping back into the hardened area she'd worked so hard to escape from filled her with dread.

"So, is that a yes?" he questioned optimistically, then took a sip of his merlot. "You should be done with the BMW campaign by then, so it'll be perfect timing."

He studied her face intently as she sat, picking at her food in silent deliberation. One of her biggest fears had always been mothering a child too early in life. Fate, however, had dealt her a different hand, and over the last few days, she'd come to terms with it surprisingly well. While she once recoiled at the thought, she now found a part of herself thrilled at the prospect of bringing this baby into the world. Unfortunately, it had just become painfully clear that it wasn't going to happen. No, she would absolve Zane of any guilt, regret, or resentment by going through with the abortion.

"I'd miss you too much if I didn't go with you," she finally answered with a small smile.

"And I'd miss you too much if you didn't come!" he said without skipping a beat.

Jenna couldn't help but feel a twinge of disappointment. Zane was normally so in tune with her, yet he didn't seem to be picking up on her anguish. She ascribed it to his excitement regarding the expansion mixed with the wine he'd been indulging in since the beginning of the meal.

"I have a little something for you," he grinned, reaching into his suit jacket and pulling a small, black box from its inner pocket.

"What's this?" Jenna asked curiously as he slid it across the candlelit table to her.

"Open it," he insisted, his big, blue eyes basking in her look of puzzlement.

"Zane, what did you do…" she blushed, realizing she was holding a jewelry box.

"Just open it," he chuckled while she held the small felt box in her trembling hands. She flashed him a nervous glance and cracked it open slowly.

"Oh my God," she gasped, a hand covering her agape mouth as she as took in the beauty of the exquisite necklace inside. "Oh my God," she repeated, unable to take her eyes off the three large, round diamonds shimmering on the white gold drop pendant that hung from a matching white gold chain. Losing her ability to speak, she looked up at him with large, watery eyes, and he returned her gaze with one of satisfied relief.

"I take it you like it," he smiled wide while she admired the necklace again with a look of stunned disbelief.

"Baby, it's… it's gorgeous!" she gushed. "It's too much, though!"

"Nonsense," he waved dismissively. "You're worth every penny and a whole lot more."

"You need every penny for the East Coast office!" she reminded him with a look of concern.

"Quiet, you," he laughed, rounding the table to help her with her new necklace. She'd been wearing her usual heart pendant but quickly removed it and slipped it into her purse before holding her long hair up so he could clasp the breathtaking showpiece around her neck. His lips met hers for a heated kiss, and he returned to his seat to watch the diamonds sparkle in the table's candlelight.

"When did you have time to do this?" she asked in awe as she held the drop pendant between her fingers to admire it again.

"Let's just say you're not the only one who left work early today," he winked.

"Sweetie, you shouldn't have done this!" Jenna persisted and gave him another look of concern.

"Honestly, even with Phil's financial blow, the company's doing just fine. I have everything under control," Zane reassured her. "Besides, this is long overdue. On our first date here, you told me about the necklace you had to pawn. That one your grandmother gave you?"

"You remembered that?" Jenna asked in shock.

"Of course I did, babe," he smiled and added sweetly, "I figured you needed something nice to hand down to your granddaughter, too."

His words reminded her of the baby she was carrying and how it would never grow old enough to have a child of its own. The key to her becoming a grandmother was living inside her, but only for a few more days. The heartbreaking thought flooded her with emotion, and she burst into tears, sobbing uncontrollably into her napkin in an attempt to hide her face in shame.

"Hey, hey, hey, what's wrong?" Zane rocketed out of his seat to wrap a strong arm around her heaving shoulders.

"N-n-n-nothing," she lied, rivulets of mascara running down her flushed cheeks.

"It doesn't look like nothing," he worried as he rubbed her back soothingly. "What did I say?"

"Seriously, nothing," she sniffed, wiping her eyes and collecting herself with a deep breath. "This is just the sweetest thing anybody's ever done for me," she deflected. Internally, a deep conflict was beginning to tear her apart. She knew abortion would be best for the immediate growth of Zane's company, but she prided herself in her honesty and didn't know if she had what it took to lie to him.

"Well, you deserve it," he told her as he brushed the hair from her face and kissed her softly on the forehead.

"I'm sorry, I didn't mean to embarrass us," she replied meekly. She glanced around the restaurant and realized several of its affluent patrons had taken notice of her outburst.

"You could never embarrass me," he comforted her with a warm smile and equally warm eyes.

"We can get out of here if you want," she sniffled.

"And miss out on dessert and your news?" he reminded her, satisfied that she'd regained herself and retaken his seat.

"Oh, that," she muttered, recalling the news she wouldn't share with him anymore.

"It's your turn to spill," he began, "but we can wait until we order dessert."

"It's nothing compared to your news," she dismissed with another lie, "I just wanted to tell you I finalized the art for the BMW campaign."

"Ah, that's wonderful news!" Zane burst happily, raising his glass in a solitary salute and finishing the rest of his wine.

A wave of guilt washed over Jenna as she looked across the table at the amazing man she was so blessed to have in her life. He treated her like a princess, appreciated her body and soul, showed her nothing but respect, even jump-starting her career…

and she'd been withholding the truth from him all week. Worse, she planned on lying to him about the termination of their unborn baby.

She was crazy about the guy and came to the sudden realization that concealing the abortion may be the be fastest way to lose him from her life. She'd always followed her heart and done what was right, and couldn't bring herself to stray from her morality now. She'd have to tell Zane, even if it meant losing him.

"I have some other news, too," she confessed sullenly. "I should have told you sooner, and I'm sorry I didn't. "

"Oh?" Zane's face grew uneasy at Jenna's abrupt change of demeanor.

"I know the timing is awful, and I really hope it doesn't mess things up too badly, but I found out..." she hesitated as she mustered the courage to finish the sentence, "I found out I'm pr—"

"Pow, pow!"

The familiar voice sounded loudly through the restaurant, interrupting her admission at its most critical moment. Jenna instantly recognized the easily identifiable catchphrase of the last person she ever wanted to see again. She followed Zane's annoyed glare across the room to the full bar located on the other side.

They weren't the only patrons who'd turned to find the source of the disturbance, the cause revealing itself to be an extremely drunk Phil Miller who sat holding a raised shot glass while rambunctiously toasting nobody in particular. The bartender, a slender, middle-aged woman with short blond hair, flashed him an irritated look, and members of the bustling wait staff even paused to scowl at his inappropriate behavior. He threw his head back and gulped down the libation, then slammed the empty glass down on the bar top while belting out another, "Pow, pow!"

"Ugh," Zane groaned as they watched the bartender lean in and whisper something in Phil's ear. Phil looked apologetic, implying the woman had asked him to keep his boisterous voice down.

"Really?" Jenna grumbled in agitation. "Of all nights?"

They'd seen Phil here before and knew he was a regular of the posh Italian eatery. He'd once intruded on their dinner by following them to their table and rudely inviting himself to eat with them. He insisted a waiter bring an extra chair and spent the meal oblivious to their frustration as he incessantly rambled on. He typically stuck to the bar, knowing it was the ideal place to schmooze with the city's deepest pockets.

They didn't expect to see him here on the same day he'd been unceremoniously let go from the job he'd held so dear, and by the looks of things, he was attempting to drink his woes away. The bartender refilled his shot glass, and he downed this one without making a spectacle of himself.

He was still wearing the same gray suit he'd been fired in, necktie now loosened and the top few buttons of his dress shirt undone, and he'd chosen to replace the unsightly medical gauze on his balding head with a smaller, flesh-colored bandage that was still quite noticeable.

"Unbelievable," an appalled Zane remarked.

"Let's just get out of here," Jenna sighed, using a hand to shield her eyes from Phil. Seeing him had upset her sensitive stomach, and she was beginning to feel queasy.

"The way he's pounding 'em back, I'm sure they'll stop serving him soon, and he'll find another place to drink," Zane observed as Phil motioned for another shot. He swallowed this one as quickly as the previous two and drunkenly swayed his bar stool.

"I really don't want to wait," Jenna huffed. "Let's just leave. We can do dessert when we get home."

"Okay, babe, we can do that. I'd rather not look at that clown anymore, either," Zane conceded as he dug his wallet out of his back pocket and dropped a crisp one-hundred dollar bill on the table.

They'd spent nearly every day together for the last three months, yet his chivalry hadn't faltered in the least. He politely helped her from her seat as she slung her purse strap over her shoulder, and she continued to shield her face from Phil while they quickly moved towards the restaurant's exit. They'd made it halfway across the dining room floor when Phil's unmistakable voice rang out loudly again.

"Hey! Hey! Zane! Jenna!"

Once more, several of the establishment's socialites turned to sneer at the disheveled drunk with the loud mouth, but Zane and Jenna pretended not to hear his calls. They ignored him as they hurried across the room, but he managed to stagger from his seat at the bar and intercept them before they made it out of the main dining area.

"Pow, pow!" he bellowed as he blocked their path with a smile, his hands forming their ridiculous makeshift guns. "Don't you two look adorable," he slurred. He looked Jenna up and down and added, "That's a pretty dress."

"Thank you," she mumbled, realizing the vibrant red dress was likely why Phil spotted them. With hiding her face no longer necessary, she dropped her hand to Zane's and clenched it tightly.

"We were just on our way out, Phil, but you have a good night," Zane nodded.

"Okay, I'll see you in the office on Monday," Phil casually replied as if the day's events had never occurred.

"No, you won't," Zane growled lowly, his patience clearly running thin as he attempted to move past his erstwhile protégé.

"Oh, what, because of earlier?" Phil cackled in amusement after stepping to the side to block their path for a second time. "Come on, man, forgive and forget! Let's just start over again. I'll be in on Monday, and we'll just pretend that whole unfortunate incident never happened."

"Phil, not now," Jenna hissed in agitation.

"Aw, come on!" Phil waved dismissively with a big, drunken grin plastered to his face. "I said some things. You said some things. We all said some things," he paused to turn his head and release a muffled burp. "Let's just move forward together. We're a great team."

"Not now, Phil," Zane repeated softly through gritted teeth, hoping to avoid a scene.

"Jenna, baby, talk some sense into your man here!" Phil laughed nervously with pleading eyes that were glazed over from alcohol. She refused to reply or even meet his stare, and the disgraced account manager took offense to both.

"Ah, go fuck yourself then, bitch!" he burst angrily.

"That's enough!" Zane demanded forcefully. His raised voice boomed over the low Sicilian music pumping through the restaurant, and a hushed silence began to fall over the dining room. Jenna tightened her grip on his strong hand and looked around the room with a fake smile to assure the growing number of onlookers that the situation was under control. "You've

embarrassed yourself enough for one day," he seethed as his composure crumbled.

"You can go fuck yourself, too!" Phil spat with a hateful sneer, and a collective gasp was heard throughout the room as he proceeded to shove his middle finger in his former boss's face. Zane swatted it away and pushed by him with Jenna clinging to his hand tightly.

"Yeah, you run away. Go run home and fuck your ghetto girlfriend," Phil scoffed. "Go fuck your little nigg—"

Zane didn't give him a chance to finish. With no warning and with lightning-fast speed, he turned and silenced the man with a right hook to the jaw. The blow was so powerful that it sent Phil careening backward into a table that fell to the floor along with him. The small group of aging women surrounding the table, all dressed in similar pantsuits, shrieked as their dinner crashed to the tile below.

Primavera's manager, a husky Italian man wearing a black suit and sporting a thick, black beard, bolted from the kitchen to address the commotion with a look of horror. Zane towered menacingly, his chest heaving from adrenaline, while Jenna stood behind him with her hands cupped over her mouth from the shock of what she'd just witnessed.

Phil lay unconscious beside the toppled table, his gray suit stained with pasta sauce, the bandage on his head having flown off at some point during his fall and leaving his grotesque stitches exposed. The restaurant's usual evening banter had been reduced to quiet mumbles as the crowd continued to watch the scene unfolding before them.

"Mr. Talbot!" the manager exclaimed in a heavy Italian accent as he assessed the damage with confusion. "What happened?"

"I'm… I'm sorry, Anthony," Zane stammered with a look of sincere apology. He glanced down at his right fist, still clenched in anger, then at Phil's crumpled body, and finally around the room at their captive audience. Behind him, Jenna began wheezing, the excitement having triggered her asthma, and reached into her purse to retrieve her inhaler.

"It's okay, everybody! Enjoy your meals while we take care of things here!" the manager announced with an embarrassed chuckle before kneeling to check on Phil's limp body. Members of the wait staff rushed to his aid, righting the table and frantically cleaning the mess from the floor while apologizing to the unimpressed women whose meal had been ruined. A waiter bent to whisper something into the manager's ear, and he looked alarmed by the news. Rising to his feet, he hurried over to Zane to relay what he'd just learned.

"You need to leave now," he spoke softly so nobody could overhear. "Somebody called the cops. They'll be here soon."

"It wasn't his fault!" Jenna pleaded in Zane's defense.

"Anthony, you know I'd never—" Zane began, only to be hastily quieted.

"Shhh… I know, old friend," the manager interrupted with a compassionate smile. "That guy's become a real nuisance here lately. I'm sure you gave him what was coming to him."

Jenna was relieved to learn that the two knew and respected each other. It was obvious by their rapport that they had some sort of history and that Anthony was eager to help Zane out of this mess.

"We'll send you a check for the damages, okay?" Jenna chimed in. Zane nodded his agreement as he wrapped his arm around her waist.

"I don't think a broken plate and three shattered wine glasses constitute 'damages,' my dear," Anthony laughed heartily. "I'll comp those women their meals and that'll be that."

"At least let me pay for those," Zane insisted, reaching for his wallet.

"Nonsense," Anthony refused. "You've done so much business with us over the years. I should be comping your meal!" he laughed again, and Jenna found his endearing, cheerful attitude to be quite calming. Behind him, the room had come alive with conversation again as the city's most influential citizens returned to their dinners. Phil had regained consciousness, groaning in pain while holding his throbbing jaw, and had managed to erect himself with the assistance of two waiters.

"You're so sweet," Jenna smiled in awe at the restaurateur's kindness.

"And you're so beautiful!" he playfully winked with innocent Italian flirtation. "Now, you two lovebirds, get out of here before the police show up."

"Thank you," Zane replied, shaking the man's hand in appreciation. Jenna had stepped behind him again as they readied themselves to leave the restaurant.

"Look out!" a shrill voice screamed from one of the tables.

Zane looked over Anthony's shoulder just in time to see Phil charging at him with a maniacal look in his eyes and wielding one of the dining room's sturdy iron chairs. He was holding it with both hands, one on its back and one on its seat, and its four metal legs protruded forward dangerously.

With little time to react, he pushed Anthony out of the way and jumped aside, failing to realize Jenna's unfortunate position. The restaurant came alive with a mixture of shocked gasps and screams as one of the chair's legs was driven into her abdomen, knocking her backward onto the floor painfully hard.

Realizing what he'd done, Phil dropped the chair and stood over Jenna's body with a look of horror. Anthony, a powerful man in his own right, wrapped a thick arm around Phil's neck and threw him to the ground. He pinned him there by placing a knee on his back and pressing down with all his weight as Zane rushed to Jenna's side. She lay writhing in agony, holding her stomach with her eyes clenched tightly as sobs of pain escaped her gritted teeth.

"Babe! Babe! Are you okay?" Zane asked in alarm. He knelt beside her and slid a hand under her back to gently lift her into a seated position. Glancing at a subdued Phil, he shot him a hateful scowl as he cradled Jenna in his arms. Anthony nodded a tacit assurance that he wouldn't be releasing Mr. Miller anytime soon.

"It hurts," Jenna groaned, holding her stomach.

"I'm calling an ambulance," Zane bleated as he reached into his suit jacket for his cell phone.

"No," Jenna stopped him, fighting to overcome the pain. "I'll… I'll be okay," she winced.

"Babe, you're hurt. I'm calling 911," he frantically insisted while she sat with his strong arm propping her up. He fished his phone from his pocket, but she swatted it aside in irritation.

"No!" she repeated loudly. "I'm fine. I just want to leave."

"Are you sure?" Zane questioned skeptically as she gripped his shoulder and struggled to her feet.

"I'm sure," she breathed and stole an embarrassed look at the audience that had gathered around them.

"Just get me out of here," she muttered, fixing her twisted dress.

"You poor thing!" a middle-aged woman from the crowd exclaimed as she hurried to Jenna's side to offer assistance, but Jenna declined it with a polite smile and dismissive wave.

"The cops will be here soon," Anthony, reminded them as he pressed his knee into Phil's back even harder, his big arm still wrapped around the man's neck. "You want to press charges?"

"No," Jenna blurted before Zane had a chance to respond. His surprised look suggested he would have answered differently. "Not right now. I just want to go home."

"Okay," Zane conceded with a sigh. Ignoring the crowd of onlookers, he asked Anthony to relate the events to the authorities and to send them his way should they need a statement. Several patrons compassionately showed their support, agreeing that Phil was wrong and offering to back the couple's story should they need it. Zane and Jenna thanked them for their kindness and thanked Anthony once more before leaving. Noticing her slight limp, Zane scooped Jenna into his powerful arms and carried her to the waiting town car with her arms wrapped around his neck. After delicately placing her inside and taking a seat next to her, he pulled her close, kissed her forehead, and instructed Carl to take them home.

"That guy's finished," Zane growled angrily as the car rolled out of the parking lot. "I was willing to let him walk with that money, but I'm not going to let him get away with this."

"Whatever you want to do," Jenna replied halfheartedly, more preoccupied with the growing pain in her abdomen than anything else.

"He's lucky Anthony got to him before I did," Zane continued to rant as the car returned to his foothill estate justifiably.

"Mmmhmm," Jenna agreed, still holding her aching belly.

"I'm going to make sure he gets locked away for a long—"

Jenna suddenly let out a loud wail, interrupting Zane mid-sentence as a bout of agonizing cramps stabbed through her lower abdomen. She threw her head back and released another tortured scream as her hands turned to fists and began punching the seat in pain. Jarred by her cries, Carl jerked the steering wheel but quickly regained control of the car. He craned his neck to find Jenna's face twisted in pain and Zane looking on in terror.

"Take us to the hospital!" Zane shouted in panicked distress. *"Now! Hurry!"*

"I… I don't know what's wrong…" a flushed Jenna trembled as tears rolled down her cheeks. As the cramping began to subside, she became aware of a warm wetness between her legs.

"It's going to be okay, babe," Zane tried his best to assure her while holding her hand. The metal leg of the chair had hit her hard, and he feared it may have caused some internal injury.

"Something's not right," she sobbed, looking into Zane's concerned eyes. She tugged her dress slightly and raised her hand to investigate the thick, wet warmth she felt spreading. She pulled her hand out and found her fingers covered with blood.

"Jesus…" Zane gasped in horror at the sight.

"I'm bleeding," Jenna gulped, her lips trembling and head spinning.

"Hurry the fuck up! Go, go, go!" Zane yelled at Carl in hysterics.

"It's... the baby..." Jenna mumbled, beginning to lose consciousness.

"What are you talking about? What baby?" Zane asked in concerned confusion as he gripped her hand tightly.

"Our baby... I think I just lost... our baby..." Jenna managed to mutter before passing out in his arms.

Chapter Fifteen

Jenna groggily woke to find herself in a hospital room. She found Zane seated in the corner with his head sunk, arms resting on his legs, and foot tapping anxiously.

"Baby…" she croaked as she came to.

"Hey!" he sprung from the small chair and darted across the room to take her hand in his.

"What… what happened?" she asked, taking in her surroundings. She vaguely recalled being in the back of his town car, but everything after that was a blur.

"You passed out," he explained soothingly, "in the back of the car. You passed out, but you're okay."

"There… there was blood," Jenna recalled as she stared at the ceiling, her eyes beginning to water as she remembered the baby.

"Yes," Zane sighed. He softly brushed the hair from her face and kissed her forehead, adding, "But you're okay."

She could tell by his troubled blue eyes that he was withholding something from her. For the first time since she'd met him, he looked as if he might shed a tear. He knew about the baby, and she could tell. It was written all over his face.

"The baby?" her shaky voice asked as her eyes watered with emotion. She already knew the answer but didn't want to hear it.

"You lost it," Zane told her quietly as he hung his head. "I'm sorry."

Her chest began to heave as she sobbed, her mascara staining her face as tears streamed down her cheeks. She wept inconsolably as Zane held her hand, his eyes now puffy and red as he shared in her grievance.

"Why didn't you tell me?" he whispered when she calmed down enough to speak.

"I... I didn't want to get in the way," she sniffled. Zane handed her his pocket square, and she wiped her eyes with the handkerchief.

"Get in the way?"

"Get in the way of your business," Jenna answered. "Especially with the expansion and everything. I didn't want to screw things up for you."

"You wouldn't have gotten in the way," Zane replied, calmingly running his fingers through her long hair. "That's silly."

"Yes, I would have," she insisted. "You worked so hard for this New York branch. Years, even. There's no way a baby wouldn't have messed it all up. That's why I was going to get an a-a-bo…," she stammered and abruptly broke eye contact with him.

"Get a what?" he gently prodded. When she remained silent, he asked again with a more soothing tone. "You were going to get a what?"

"I was going to get an abortion," she confessed in a mumble, ashamed to speak the words aloud. "The appointment was next week."

"You were going to get an abortion without even telling me you were pregnant?" Zane asked in appalling.

"I didn't know what to do! I planned on telling you tonight, I swear," Jenna pleaded. "I was trying to tell you, but then Phil…"

"I know, I know," Zane sighed. "I just can't believe you even thought about aborting our baby…"

"You wouldn't have wanted me to?"

"Of course not!" he fired back. "Don't you understand how much I care about you? I would have been by your side every step of the way. New York could have waited."

"I'm so sorry," she swallowed hard, embarrassed by her assumptions and sensing a disappointment in Zane. She could tell that she'd violated his trust and had hurt him deeply in doing so. He consoled her with another gentle kiss on her forehead and stayed with her throughout the night. She was released the following morning, and the two spoke very little as Carl drove them back to the foothill estate that now felt cold and unwelcoming to her.

Over the following weeks, Jenna withdrew from Zane, becoming distant after her tragic miscarriage. They'd both given their statements to the police, and Phil had been charged with aggravated assault. They heard nothing more from him as he awaited trial, and when the day arrived, their court testimony put him away for two years. It would have been one, but a sympathetic judge agreed that the loss of Jenna's baby warranted a longer stay.

Zane realized Jenna's worst fear by postponing the New York expansion and choosing to stay with her in Tucson to support her emotional healing. Although he denied it, she feared he resented her for delaying the launch of his East Coast branch and found herself growing increasingly despondent. She'd taken a week-long absence from work in the aftermath of her loss, leaving Zane to present BMW with the campaign she'd worked so diligently on. They loved the bold new strategy she'd helped create and eagerly agreed to run with it.

When she did return to the firm, wading through a sea of condolences, her work suffered noticeably from the deep depression she'd sunk into. Her creative faucet that once flowed so freely had been reduced to a trickle, and she found the sympathetic looks from her coworkers too much to bear.

She could feel their eyes on her and could hear the murmurs behind her back. Zane was relieved when she requested more time off and happily granted her as much as she needed. He'd been against her returning so quickly in the first place, insisting she wasn't ready to jump back into the swing of things. The entire place reminded her of Phil Miller and kept the painful memory of her assault and subsequent miscarriage at the forefront of her mind.

Their relationship began to decay, guilt overcoming Jenna and driving a wedge between her and Zane. He tried his best to cheer her up, but every attempt failed. The beautiful memories of their magical first date at *Primavera* had now been overwritten by the horrible recollections of her miscarriage, ruining the restaurant for the both of them forever. She began to have reoccurring nightmares of the incident, waking up terrified yet shunning Zane's efforts to console her. She was ashamed of herself for even considering the termination, and knowing Zane would have welcomed the baby filled her with remorse. Weeks later, she still felt as if he judged her for scheduling the abortion without his knowledge and suspected he harbored resentment for having to push back the launch of the New York office.

Her worry resulted in tension between them that caused their living situation to grow uncomfortable. She considered moving out, but Leigh had found a new roommate and wasn't thrilled about living alone.

The decision of where to live came when she received an unexpected phone call from her brother informing her that their mother had fallen ill. She'd been diagnosed with terminal cancer, and her frequent hospital visits explained why Jenna hadn't heard much from her. The woman hadn't wanted to worry her daughter about her sickness, choosing to remain silent as her health deteriorated. According to her brother, she didn't have much time left. As much as she dreaded returning to her old neighborhood, she knew she had to be there for her mother's final days.

She packed her things into the car Zane had bought her as he watched in sadness. He understood why she needed to go and pleaded to accompany her, but they both knew the time apart would do them good. Deep down, she felt there was no salvaging their damaged relationship. She could tell by his sad eyes, as he watched her stuff most of her belongings into the vehicle, that he suspected this goodbye was likely permanent.

After an emotional goodbye, she made the 2,400-mile journey back across the country in only three days, this time without issue and with plenty of money in her bank account thanks to the bonus she'd received for her work on the BMW campaign.

Back in Brooklyn, she stayed by her mother's bedside, caring for her as the cancer got progressively worse until she passed in her sleep four weeks later. Her brother attended the small funeral with her, where the two grieved together over the woman who'd sacrificed so much to keep food in their bellies and clothes on their backs. She chose to stay in New York

City, fearing it was too soon to return to the Southwest, and used her savings to move to a much better neighborhood in a different borough. Her mother's death also strengthened her sense of family, and she wanted to spend more time with her brother. He was still spending his time with the wrong crowd, and she hoped she could help get his life on track before he wound up in prison or the morgue.

Communication between her and Zane dwindled as they both struggled to move on with their lives. The phone calls stopped, as did the text messages and e-mails. Still, she thought about him daily and appreciated the recommendation he'd given that helped her land a job with *Regency Advertising*, an up-and-coming marketing firm based out of Manhattan. She fit in well with the start-up company and found her creativity returning as memories of her pregnancy faded and her reoccurring nightmares stopped.

She excelled at her job, quickly moving up the ranks to become the head of the art department, and her coworkers all seemed to adore her. As weeks turned to months, her career blossomed, and her social circle grew with it. She still kept in touch with Leigh fairly regularly, along with a few other acquaintances from Tucson via social media, but had made a few good friends at her new firm and found her desire to move back to Arizona waning. She missed Zane terribly but had settled into a new life and was managing her asthma well enough.

She began to hear rumblings in the workplace of a potential buyout, but management remained tight-lipped and would neither confirm nor deny the rumors.

Two weeks after the whispers started circulating, she arrived to find a meeting had been called in the firm's small conference room, where all twenty employees had gathered to hear the announcement they'd already anticipated. The small company had been sold, and the buyer would introduce himself shortly. After a brief rundown of the restructuring, management stepped back to let the new owner greet the team. Jenna's mouth fell open in disbelief as Zane Talbot, looking every bit as breathtaking as she remembered him, entered the room to a round of light applause. He spotted her immediately, flashing her a wink and a small smirk as he made his way to the front of the room to present himself.

After expounding on the buyout and explaining that the firm was now a division of *Enterprise Marketing*, Zane shared a bit of information about himself before making his way around the room to politely shake hands with his new employees. His blue eyes lit up when he felt her touch, and her heart immediately began to flutter in his presence. Months had passed since she'd seen him, yet she felt as giddy as she had almost one year earlier when they'd first met. Her pulse raced as they silently stared into each other's eyes with a warm smile for a long moment before he moved on to the next employee.

Zane took the time to assure everyone that the changes meant better job security and an increased salary and to respond to their individual questions and concerns. He made a powerful first impression, leaving the crew delighted with the company's direction. Jenna wasn't surprised that everybody instantly liked the charming man she'd once called a lover.

None of them knew of their history, as she hadn't felt the need to share it with anyone. She knew talking about him would only make her miss him much more, and she didn't need her emotions to affect her work again.

With the meeting reaching its end, the team dispersed back to their designated departments while Jenna and Zane lingered behind in the conference room. He closed the door to give them the necessary privacy before turning to her with a nervous grin.

"So…" he began cautiously, "surprised?"

"Um, yeah," she answered with a slight chuckle. "You could say that."

"Not as surprised as I was when I saw your name on the payroll!" Zane laughed in relief as he wrapped his arms around her in an affectionate embrace. "I've missed you," he sighed, stepping back and touching her shoulders. He stood looking deep into her eyes, and she sensed he may be fighting back tears. She knew she certainly was; it was a battle she didn't think she could win. She felt her eyes begin to well and her lips tremble as old feelings rushed to the surface.

"So, wait, you didn't know I worked here?" she asked while attempting to gain control of herself.

"Not initially, no," he shook his head. "I was in the middle of the purchase when I glanced at the employee roster and spotted your name. It was a pleasant surprise. I took it as a sign that I was making the right move."

"I can't believe you bought the entire company!" she blurted in amazement. "How did you—"

"I know, I know," he stopped her, knowing what she was going to ask. Although *Regency Advertising* was a small firm, it had been doing quite well, and the purchase hadn't been cheap. "After you left, I used work to fill the void. I refocused all of my attention solely on business and snagged a few high-paying clients. Phil's replacement has been a big help, too. You'd like her."

"That's great," she smiled. "But those new clients were enough to buy out Regency?"

"Well, not exactly..." he trailed off and cleared his throat as he fidgeted with his necktie.

"Oh, no. Zane, what did you do?" she asked in concern. It was quite obvious that he was holding something from her.

"I sold the estate," he confessed.

"Wait, what? You sold the house?" Jenna questioned in shock. She knew how much he loved that home and how hard he'd worked to have it built to his exact specifications.

"Eh, it wasn't the same without you anyway," he told her. "Everything just reminded me of you. It was just too depressing."

"I can't believe you sold it. That's... wow. Where are you living now?"

"Here, now," he replied. "I rented a nice loft downtown. I finish moving in this week. It's a one-year lease, so I'll be here for a while. It'll give me time to oversee the transition and get things running smoothly."

"Then you're heading back to Tucson?"

"More than likely," he shrugged. "Phil's replacement says she'd have no problem moving here to manage this branch."

"Well," she sighed, "looks like we'll be working together again."

As the reality set in, she wasn't sure how she felt about the situation. She would now be working for her ex-lover, the man whose baby she'd lost and the man who she was still very much in love with. Intuitive as always, he picked up on her apprehension and realized his surprise wasn't as well received as he'd hoped.

"I'm sorry," he said apologetically in the deep voice she'd missed so much. "I should have told you sooner. I shouldn't have sprung it on you like this."

"It's okay…" she muttered, breaking eye contact to look around the room nervously.

"No, it's not. I don't know what I was thinking. I just missed you so much," he replied, his cool composure beginning to crack, revealing his emotions.

"You did?" she asked with a hint of skepticism.

"You have no idea," he choked as his eyes began to water. For the first time, he was showing a vulnerability she'd never seen, and the sight of his aching heart also brought tears to her eyes.

"I thought you hated me…" she admitted.

"What?" he gasped at the absurd notion. "Jenna, I could never hate you."

"But the whole abortion thing," she paused, the painful memory stabbing her, "and the expansion, which I totally screwed up…"

"Babe," he took her hand in his and spoke earnestly into her big, brown eyes, "You don't get it, do you?"

"Get what?" she swallowed hard, looking back at his intent face.

"I'm in love with you," he burst as a tear streamed down his cheek. "I've been in love with you since the first moment I saw you."

"You… you are?" she stammered, taken aback by his spontaneous admission.

"I'm so in love with you, Jenna Parker, and I should have told you sooner. Hell, I wanted to tell you after the first week," he chuckled anxiously. "I don't know why I waited so damn long. I was just scared, I think. I've never said those words before."

"I love you, too," she sobbed in the joy of finally speaking the words she'd been holding back for so long.

"Yeah?" he asked as the widest smile she'd ever seen stretched across his face. He wrapped his strong arms around her waist and quickly pulled her close.

"Yeah," she giggled and echoed his confession as she wiped his tears away, "since the first moment I saw you."

Their lips met in a long, passionate kiss with total disregard for anyone who may oversee through the door's small window. In this moment, they were completely lost in each other, and nobody else existed but them.

"The way you left so suddenly..." he whispered when their lips finally parted, "I assumed you just wanted to be left alone."

"Silly man," she smiled as she ran her long fingers through his dark hair. "I've thought about you every day."

"I knew you needed some time, but I thought you might not want to see me again," he explained.

"I just felt so guilty about everything..." she muttered, lowering her head.

"Don't ever feel guilty for a second," he insisted. He lifted her chin to kiss her again. "Turns out pushing the expansion back was a blessing in disguise anyway," he assured her.

"Oh?" she questioned with her brow raised in curiosity.

"Remember that cheap office space I told you I found a few months ago?"

"Yes?"

"Turns out there was a reason it was so cheap. Huge rodent infestation. I found out the whole building was condemned," he laughed.

"Jesus," she gasped, the news already alleviating some of her guilt.

"Thanks to that delay, I was able to come up with the money to just buy out Regency," he grinned. "Expanded and knocked out some competition all in one blow, see?"

"Maybe everything does happen for a reason," she smiled. He leaned in for another kiss but stopped short when he noticed the chain around her neck.

"Is that what I think it is?" he asked, pulling the necklace out from her sweater and revealing the diamond drop pendant he'd given her moments before their world fell apart.

"It is," she blushed as he held the pendant in his hand.

"I'm so glad you kept it," he sniffled as another tear escaped his eye.

"I wear it every day," she stated proudly, wiping his tears away again with her thumb.

"It doesn't remind you of…"

He stopped himself from mentioning the horrific incident. He didn't need to speak the words for her to know what he meant.

"No," she answered truthfully. "It reminds me of you. And I still want to hand it down to my granddaughter."

"Our granddaughter," he corrected her with a playful smile.

Speechless and overcome with joy, she touched his cheeks and pulled his lips to hers again.

"I love you," she purred as they exchanged another long, heated kiss.

"I love you, too," he breathed, tightening his arms around her waist and bringing her closer to him.

They'd found each other again, and their love reignited with a flame that would never be extinguished. This time, nothing would keep them apart.

Epilogue

The years to come saw *Enterprise Marketing* become a publicly-traded corporation. When it landed in the Fortune 500, Zane Talbot attributed its success to his wife, Jenna Talbot, whom he'd wed in a lavish ceremony in the foothills of Tucson, Arizona. The couple had returned there to build a life for themselves, collaborating together on the design of a new home they'd go on to raise their two children.

Zane Talbot, CEO of the powerhouse that *Enterprise Marketing* had become, continued to credit the company's prosperity to his wife, citing her creative genius as the key component in their award-winning campaigns. He also thanked the rest of his hard-working staff, rewarding them generously for their contributions and earning the nickname "World's Best CEO" by *Forbes* magazine.

Upon his release from Maricopa County Jail, Phil Miller returned to a life of alcohol, quickly blowing the money he'd embezzled on booze and prostitutes. He was struck by a car and killed in his attempt to cross a busy street while stumbling drunk. Zane and Jenna read of his death in the *Arizona Daily Star* newspaper. Both refused to attend his funeral.

Jenna cried when handing the necklace down to her granddaughter.